'Are you alwa[ys] work with?' he [...]

Rose stumbled over [...] the warmth of Dave's hand immed[iately] elbow. She shrugged him off, not caring if he thought she was rude. She was hot, dirty and tired from driving for the past two days.

'You should be wearing sensible shoes, not those strappy little fashion things.'

'Well, excuse me,' she said crossly. 'I hadn't planned on assisting in a major trauma retrieval team, and I'll thank you to keep your comments about the way I dress to yourself.'

'Difficult and snappy. Oh, the next six months are going to be a barrel of laughs.'

Rose glared at him. 'Listen, Dave whoever-you-are, I'm hot, uncomfortable and extremely tired. Now, if you want my help then get… off…my…back.'

Dave was frowning at her. 'Let's get to hospital,' he said briskly, before striding off towards the ambulance.

What was the matter with him? He was a grown man and one look at Miss High and Mighty had his hormones in overdrive. Keep your mind on the job. That was the answer, and it was the best advice he could give himself.

Lucy Clark began writing romance in her early teens and immediately knew she'd found her 'calling' in life. After working as a secretary in a busy teaching hospital, she turned her hand to writing medical romance. She currently lives in South Australia with her husband and two children. Lucy largely credits her writing success to the support of her husband, family and friends.

You can visit Lucy's website at www.lucyclark.net or e-mail her at lucyclark@optusnet.com.au

Recent titles by the same author:

THE OUTBACK DOCTOR

BY
LUCY CLARK

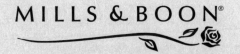

MILLS & BOON®

To Pete, My own hero. My one true love.
Song of Songs 1:2

First published in Great Britain 2002
Harlequin Mills & Boon Limited,
Eton House, 18-24 Paradise Road, Richmond, Surrey TW9 1SR

© Lucy Clark 2002

ISBN 0 263 83422 0

Set in Times Roman 10½ on 11 pt.
03-0103-52513

Printed and bound in Spain
by Litografía Rosés, S.A., Barcelona

CHAPTER ONE

SHE was not having fun!

Rose rested her elbow on the window-ledge and rubbed her fingers across her temple, her left hand on the steering-wheel. What had made her think that driving from Sydney to Broken Hill would be less hassle than flying and hiring a car once she arrived?

She would need to stop soon and battle the flies, due to the eighth bottle of water she'd consumed since breakfast. Drinking a lot served two purposes. She was forced to stop and revive as well as decreasing the risk of dehydrating. The weather was so stinking hot, even now, when it was approaching dusk. Well, at least there was air-conditioning in the car.

Rose heard a noise and immediately glanced in her rear-view mirror. A red sedan, with spoilers and gleaming chrome, was about to overtake her. It must be doing close to one hundred and thirty kilometres per hour as she herself was doing the State limit of one hundred.

'Idiots!' she mumbled as they roared past, the passenger in the car waving to her as they went. At this time of the evening, when the chances of hitting a kangaroo increased dramatically, speeding was the last thing on her mind. Last night, she'd made sure she'd stopped before dusk but as she was now about half an hour out of Broken Hill, she saw no point in stopping. Not if she was careful.

Rose checked the map again. Visions of using the bath-room at her father's house made her smile. Better that than a dirty, fly-ridden petrol station or worse—having to squat!

Ten minutes later, she saw the outline of a large object in the middle of the road and automatically decreased her speed. Was it a roo? She'd seen a few dead ones on the side of the road since her journey had begun and it had made her sad. Still, it was a fact of outback life—or so she'd read. No—it wasn't a roo. The silhouette was far too big.

The sun picked out a gleam of red and Rose's stomach churned. Her heartbeat accelerated and as she mentally went through a check list of what was in her medical bag, safely nestled in the back seat, she hoped she wouldn't be needing any of it.

As she neared, she saw the situation was even worse than she'd first imagined.

'Oh, no!' Rose's mouth hung open, her eyes as wide as saucers as she took in the scene before her. It was horrific!

The red car hadn't hit anything as yielding as a roo. It was on one side, the roof of the car completely buckled and hard up against the second trailer of a road train. She'd never seen a road train this close up and they were a lot longer than she'd expected. The front had hit the gravel shoulder of the road and sunk down into the drainage ditch, tipping the driver's side of the cab up so the left side was almost buried in the ground.

The trailer that was connected directly to the cab was also in the ditch but still upright. The second and third trailers were blocking the road completely. Rose swallowed the sickening jolt that had initially twisted her stomach and forced her professionalism to the fore. She picked up her mobile phone as she brought the car to a halt but found it was out of range.

'Damn!' She cut the engine and switched on her hazard lights before reaching around into the back for her medical bag and her hat. Climbing from the car, she jogged along the road towards the wreck, the hot January weather hitting her like a brick.

Dust. Petrol. Blood. Death. The smells were poignant in the air and her eyes stung with hot tears at the senseless mess before her.

As she came closer, she could see the driver of the road train lying out through the front of the cab, half in, half out of the windscreen. Dropping her bag to the ground, she grabbed hold of his wrist, checking his pulse.

She sighed with relief. It was there. It was quite strong. 'Can you hear me?' she called, but received no answer. 'I'm just going to take a quick look around and then I'll be back.'

Rose picked up her bag and headed down the road, being careful of the debris. The petrol smell became stronger as she neared the red car. She got as close as she dared, her gaze searching hard through the wreckage for the two men who'd been in there.

She could only see one—the driver—and by the way he was positioned, squashed between pieces of twisted metal, she knew he was dead. With all the broken glass around, the other person could have been thrown through the windscreen. She looked around, scanning the fairly flat vegetation for signs of life, swatting continuously at the flies.

'There.' Her heart pounded fiercely against her chest as she rushed over to where the body lay—lifeless on the fine orangey-brown dirt. He was lying face down, his legs twisted at awful angles. Just by looking at them, she could tell they were badly fractured. She dumped her bag on the ground and quickly pulled out a pair of gloves and tugged them on.

Pressing two fingers to his carotid pulse, Rose didn't like what she felt. It was thready and faint. Reaching for her medical torch, she turned his head slightly and checked his pupils. They were both sluggish.

She checked his pulse again and while her fingers were still pressed firmly to the man's neck, his pulse disappeared. 'Oh, no, you don't,' she said firmly. Turning him over, Rose checked he hadn't swallowed his tongue before grabbing an expired air resuscitation mask from her bag and placing it over the man's mouth. Tipping his head

back, she pinched his nose and breathed five quick breaths
into his mouth.

Finding the right spot just beneath the man's sternum,
she placed one hand on top of the other and laced her
fingers together before starting external cardiac compres-
sion. Rose concentrated and counted. Fifteen compressions—two breaths. She checked his pulse. Nothing. Compressions, breaths. Still no pulse. She went again and this
time when she checked for a pulse she found one.

'Good,' she puffed. 'Now let's try and see what else is
happening to you.' She glanced over her shoulder, thinking
she'd heard something, but she couldn't see anything. Her
thoughts went to the truck driver. Perhaps he'd regained
consciousness. She couldn't check him just yet as this
man's injuries were more urgent. As she was the only person around, she had the triage call as to which patient
required immediate attention.

She checked his pupils again. They were still sluggish,
the right one slightly larger than the left. Not a good sign,
she thought as she felt his limbs for breaks. She checked
his pulse again just as she heard the sound of a car. Thank
goodness. Even if the person did nothing other than get in
contact with the ambulance or Royal Flying Doctor
Service, she didn't care. She wasn't on her own any more.

The pulse disappeared again and Rose groaned. She
went through the motions again and was in the middle of
counting her cardiac compressions when the vehicle
stopped, quite close to where she was, sending dirt over
her crisp white top. Rose shut both her eyes and her mouth
for a few seconds while the dust settled, and when she
opened them, it was to find a pair of well-worn work boots,
thick socks and tanned, hairy legs in her direct line of
vision. She glanced up as the man squatted down. His hat
was wide and also well worn and hid most of his face.

''Struth!'

'Call for an ambulance or RFDS or something,' she
muttered as he crouched down.

'Already done.'

His voice was deep and rich but she didn't have time to think about such things at the moment. 'Great. Do you know CPR?'

'Sure, but I'll just go take a look around first.'

'I need you here,' she demanded, wondering if everyone in the outback was such a sticky-beak.

'You're doing fine. I won't be long.'

'Get back here,' she called in between counts but he was gone. 'Of all my luck,' she told her unconscious patient, but returned her concentration to counting the compressions.

True to his word, the stranger came back. 'You do the breaths, I'll take over the compressions,' he stated, and simply knelt down and did as he'd said, not giving her the opportunity to say a word.

They worked together. Five compressions and then Rose blew one breath into the patient's mouth.

'One, two, three, four, five, breathe,' he kept chanting.

At the end of the next set, Rose checked for the pulse. 'Nothing,' she reported. 'Let's go again.'

'No.'

'No?'

He picked up her medical torch and checked the patient's pupils. 'Fixed and dilated. I'm calling it. Time of death…' He checked his watch.

'You can't *call* it.'

'Eighteen twenty-three,' he continued as though she hadn't spoken. 'Why not?' He stood and picked up a black bag that was just off to the right of him. She hadn't seen him put it there. She glanced at her own medical bag.

'You're a doctor?'

'Obviously.' He didn't wait for her to continue with the conversation and instead took off towards the truck driver. 'Well, come on,' he called impatiently over his shoulder, and Rose bristled as she rose to her feet and grabbed her own bag.

She supposed she shouldn't look a gift horse in the mouth. She should be glad that the one person who'd arrived to help her was probably the local doctor. Rose rushed after him, knowing the truck driver needed their attention.

'I see the driver of the red car doesn't need our expertise,' the man stated when she caught up to him.

'No. Killed himself outright.' Rose looked at the truck driver. 'He's regained consciousness.'

'What makes you say that?'

'He's moved.' The driver was now almost completely out of the cab, coming across the front of the engine.

'This is where he was when I came over to take a look. Help me get him down.'

Rose worked with the doctor, glad he was there. 'I've got some morphine in my bag so that should help him with the pain.'

'Good. Get an IV line set up, stat, then check his vital signs. Bob? Bob can you hear me? It's Dave, mate.' No reply.

'How do you know him?' Rose asked.

'He's a mate of mine,' Dave mumbled, pulling on a fresh pair of gloves and taking some scissors out of his bag before cutting Bob's navy T-shirt away. His abdomen was completely covered in blood and Dave began cleaning it up with gauze swabs. 'If he's come out through the front of the cab then he would have come over the windscreen.'

'Correct.' Rose was almost finished with the IV line. The sooner Bob got these fluids into him, the better. 'He was lying over it—half in, half out—when I first checked him.'

'Why didn't you get him out?' Dave demanded.

Rose didn't like his tone at all. 'His pulse was fine and I needed to assess the status of the other two patients. I was the only one here,' she continued, her words and body language completely defensive, 'and I made the triage call. As the other patient is now dead and Bob has clearly regained consciousness and managed to get himself out of the cab, I'd say I made the right choice.'

'All right, all right. Don't get your knickers in a twist. I was only asking.'

'No. You were criticising.'

Dave was silent for a moment. 'He's got glass in here,' he said, pulling a piece from Bob's abdomen and throwing it away, his gloved hand covered in blood. 'What's his BP?'

'Eighty over forty. That's not good.'

'No joke.'

Rose continued to check Bob's vital signs as well as running her hands expertly over Bob's limbs. 'Right femur feels fractured. That can't be helping with the blood loss.'

'Right arm doesn't look good either. He's not gonna be too thrilled when he comes around.'

'Well, at least Bob is alive.'

'Still, he isn't going to be too happy.'

'I've given him some morphine, so that should at least help with his pain.'

'Good.' Once that was done, they worked together to splint Bob's broken leg, getting him ready for when the ambulance arrived. Dave kept talking to their patient all the time, telling him everything they were doing and that he was going to make it.

'So what type of doctor are you?' Dave asked as they worked.

'Anaesthetist.'

'Rose Partridge?' he queried.

'Yes.' She was momentarily taken aback.

'Just as well you're here. The other anaesthetist left this morning and the locum isn't due to arrive until tomorrow.'

'What would you have done had I not arrived until Monday?'

'We do have people who are trained to give anaesthetics but aren't anaesthetists,' he replied matter-of-factly.

'Glad to hear it.'

He tipped his head to one side and listened. Then Rose heard it, too. Sirens. 'Let's change this dressing so he's ready for the ambos.' The cavalry was coming. Rose assisted him before doing Bob's vital signs once more.

'Pupils equal and reacting to light. BP now one hundred over fifty-five. At least those fluids being pumped into him are working.'

'Yeah, but he's still losing a lot of blood.'

When the emergency crews arrived, Rose had to admit she was impressed. They may have turned up in vehicles which weren't state of the art, like the ones in Sydney, but they were functional for what needed to be done.

Once the dressing was changed, Dave ripped off his gloves and headed over to talk to the ambulance officers, or ambos as they were more affectionately known, leaving Rose to monitor Bob. He pointed in her direction and also to where the other patient was. At least they all knew who was in charge!

'G'day.' One of the ambos brought over a stretcher. 'Dave says ya the new anaesthetist.'

'That's right,' Rose replied.

'Not the best type of welcome for ya but we're all mighty glad you're here, Doc.'

'Thank you.' Rose launched into a spiel of Bob's vital statistics as the ambos got him ready to move. When he was finally being wheeled away towards the ambulance, Rose removed her gloves and locked her bag. She was hot and sticky and as she stood to brush the dirt from her crumpled white shorts, she realised she'd have to bleach not only her shorts but her top as well as the orangey-brown dirt had well and truly settled into the fabric.

She swatted the flies away frustratedly before picking up her bag and heading back to her car. Dave jogged over and fell into step with her.

'You're going the wrong way. I need you to ride with Bob in the ambulance.'

'Why can't you?'

'I'll follow in my ute.'

'Why can't I follow in my car? I'm sure the ambos are more than capable of caring for the patient during the ride to hospital.'

'He might regain consciousness again during the drive.'

'All the more reason why you should authorise some medication for him, then.'

'But you're the anaesthetist. You'll have a better idea of what analgesics he'll need.'

Rose sighed heavily. 'Fine, I'll organise some analgesics but I'm still following in my car.'

'We can get someone else to drive it to the hospital for you.'

'Then why can't we get someone to drive your ute to the hospital? After all, if Bob starts to haemorrhage, he's going to need you on hand to deal with it.'

'Are you always this difficult to work with?' Dave asked.

Rose stumbled over a stone on the road and felt the warmth of Dave's hand immediately at her elbow, steadying her. She shrugged him off, not caring if he thought she was rude. She hot, dirty and tired from driving for the past two days.

'You should be wearing sensible shoes, not those strappy little fashion things.'

'Well, excuse me,' she said crossly. 'I hadn't planned on assisting in a major trauma retrieval team and I'll thank you to keep your comments about the way I dress to yourself.'

'Difficult and snappy. Oh, the next six months are going to be a barrel of laughs.'

They'd reached Rose's car and she turned around to glare at him. 'Listen, Dave whoever-you-are, I have been driving for two days to get to Broken Hill. I'm hot, uncomfortable and extremely tired. Now, if you want my help then get…off…my…back!' Rose glared at him, adding emphasis to the last four words. Then she turned and opened her door, placing her medical bag carefully on the seat. Next, she took a white handkerchief from her pocket and took off her hat, wiping the perspiration from her forehead and running her fingers through her short blonde hair.

She'd half expected Dave to have gone, but when she turned around again it was to find him frowning at her as though she were some sort of alien. 'Let's check on Bob and then get to the hospital,' he said briskly, before striding off towards the ambulance.

What was the matter with him? He was a grown man and one look at Miss High and Mighty had his hormones in overdrive. So she was beautiful—he'd fallen in love with beautiful before and where had it got him? Divorced!

'Just concentrate on your patient and keep your mouth shut, Dunbar,' he mumbled.

'Talking to yaself, Dave?' one member of the emergency crews asked. They were getting ready to spray the road, dampening any petrol fumes that might ignite before they began the tedious job of cutting the body from the wreck. The young man who they'd tried to resuscitate was being taken care of by the local undertakers who'd arrived on the scene soon after the ambulance.

'Something like that. Keep up the good work,' he encouraged, but continued on his way to the ambulance. He could feel rather than see that Rose was following him, which annoyed him even more. Keep your mind on the job. That was the answer and it was the best advice he could give himself.

Once he reached the ambulance, he climbed in and assessed Bob's condition. For now, he was as stabilised as they could get him.

As Rose climbed in, Dave could smell the subtle scent of her perfume and was surprised that it wasn't as overpowering as that which most city girls usually wore. It was sleek and seductive, winding its way around him and drawing him closer. He shook his head to clear it and handed her Bob's chart.

'If you authorise some analgesics, we'll get this show on the road.'

'Certainly, Doctor,' she replied briskly, and, without waiting for her, Dave climbed from the ambulance and spoke to the ambos.

When everyone was ready, they shut the back door of the ambulance and headed back to their respective vehicles. Dave found the urge was too great and couldn't resist looking over his shoulder to where Rose hurried towards her car. Her back was ramrod straight, her arms swinging at her sides, her hips swaying slightly. The action was unintentionally provocative and once more Dave had to rein in his hormones.

He kept a close eye on her in his rear-view mirror as they followed the ambulance back into town. Her sporty Jaguar XJ-6 kept up quite nicely with the ambulance and his ute, and he couldn't help reflecting that the woman and machine complemented each other nicely.

Finally, they arrived at the hospital without the need to stop, Bob's situation remaining stable. Dave had kept in constant contact with the ambos, via the HF radio, the entire way. Now they'd arrived, it was all systems go.

As he walked in the door, he called for Carrie, one of the theatre nurses. 'Dr Rose Partridge, the new anaesthetist, is about to walk through those doors. Show her where she needs to be, changing rooms, theatres—that sort of thing.'

'No problem, Dave.'

He strode to Bob's side and asked for an update on vital signs, and was glad to hear his mate was hanging in there. 'Cross-type and match. Two units of blood, stat. Let's get him to X-ray,' Dave said as he wrote up the requests for Radiology. 'I'll be in Theatre, getting things ready. Page me when he's done.' With that he headed for the male changing rooms to get ready. Once he was changed, he walked out into the corridor, only to find Rose standing there, looking slightly lost. She was dressed in theatre scrubs.

She even looked good in baggy blue cotton, he realised, but knew he shouldn't have been surprised. She seemed the type of woman who would look good in a garbage bag. Her hair was slightly wet, indicating she'd had a quick shower to get all that dirt off her before she'd changed into the scrubs.

He stood by the door and stared.

When she turned and caught him in the act, he found he couldn't move. For what seemed like an endless moment they looked at each other, and Dave felt his breath catch in his throat. Her deep blue eyes were made brighter by the blue of the material. She was…a vision.

Rose was first to break the contact, looking down at the ground momentarily before walking off. She didn't care which direction she went but she knew she couldn't stay still any longer. With one single look, Dave had managed to increase her heartbeat so it pounded erratically against her ribs. Her knees felt like jelly and her mind seemed incapable of coherent thought.

Why should she be feeling slightly breathless just because she'd shared a look with Dave Whoever? So what if he'd made her a little breathless and light-headed with the scorching look that had seemed to reach right down into the depths of her soul? He probably looked at every woman like that. Learn from your experiences, she told herself. All men were awful and that was all there was to it.

'The heat,' she mumbled. She just wasn't used to the heat. When she finally found which theatre Bob was due to be in, she was told that the patient was still in Radiology but that Dave had asked to be paged when Bob returned. Rose frowned. Why would Dave want to know? Shouldn't the surgeon in charge be informed? The pennies started to drop and she realised that Dave *was* the surgeon and not a local GP, as she'd originally thought.

Her opinion of him grew a little—a very little. He was conceited, arrogant and dictatorial. All the qualities she'd come to expect from a surgeon. She was quite surprised she hadn't picked up on it sooner. Then again, she *had* been a little preoccupied since they'd met.

When they eventually were under way in Theatre, Rose re-evaluated her opinion of him yet again. As far as his professional attributes went, they were superb. He was casual yet direct with his staff and possessed great skill as a surgeon.

The man seemed to have many facets to his personality, at least from what she'd observed during the past few hours, and part of her was intrigued by that. She monitored the patient, keeping a close eye on the dials, forcing any personal thoughts of Dave Whoever out of her mind.

Dave methodically went through the steps to stop the bleeding, suturing off the offending arteries in the femur and removing glass from Bob's abdomen but leaving the fractured bone for the orthopod to fix. Nevertheless, he didn't close the wound until he was absolutely positive each and every piece of shattered glass had been removed.

When he was finished, Rose accompanied the patient to Recovery, ensuring that Bob didn't have any side-effects from the anaesthetic. She wrote up her notes and went to change back into her dirty clothes, longing to get to her father's house so she could have a more leisurely shower.

After she'd dressed, she returned to Recovery to find Dave sitting by Bob's bed, talking softly to his friend. She was just to the side of him so he couldn't really see her, and it gave her the opportunity to observe him further.

'Hang in there, mate,' he said softly. 'I know last year was a horrible year for you, and you didn't need this to happen, but you're going to get through it, mate. Promise.'

Rose felt her heart melt at the genuine concern Dave felt for his friend.

'I've done a first-rate job on you, mate,' he continued. 'Everything's going to be smelling of roses once we get your orthopaedic bits taken care of. You'll be as good as new.'

Rose continued to stare at Dave. Who was he? First she'd thought he'd been some busybody come to gawk at the accident. Then she'd discovered he was a doctor. Not only a doctor but Broken Hill's resident general surgeon.

Now here he was, displaying compassion for his friend, the friend he'd operated on and, more than likely, saved his life. From what she could tell, Bob's internal injuries were not a pretty sight yet Dave had systematically gone about making sure everything was back where it was supposed to be.

It must have been extremely difficult to operate on his friend, but when he'd been standing at the operating table he'd been one hundred per cent professional. Rose had never been in that type of situation before—anaesthetising and monitoring a friend—yet she supposed that, being the only general surgeon in Broken Hill, he would have to do it quite often.

Thankfully, Bob's fractured femur and arm were stabilised and she wondered whether he'd be transported to Adelaide, six hours away, for orthopaedic treatment or whether someone at the hospital would perform the surgery.

It was all quite new to her, working in a small hospital. She was so used to the red tape of a large teaching hospital that she knew it might take her some time to adjust to the way things were done in this eighty-eight-bed hospital.

As she stood by the door, watching him, Rose felt the stirrings of admiration. It was strange. She usually took her time to get to know new acquaintances before admiration set in—if the person was worthy of the label. Other people usually thought her stand-offish at first, until they discovered the real Rose lying beneath the cool exterior, but because Julian had broken her heart and crushed her self-confidence, Rose had built many walls around her for protection.

'Problem?'

Rose snapped out of her reverie and realised that Dave was now looking at her.

'Uh—no problem,' she spluttered. 'I just didn't want to intrude.'

The frown in Dave's forehead deepened.

'How's he doing?' she continued as she crossed to the end of the bed and picked up the chart. She pretended to read it, knowing it was only a matter of five minutes since she'd last read it. No other changes had been made but, still, she had to do something to escape his penetrating gaze.

'Same.' He stood and walked around behind her. As he passed, Rose caught a whiff of his aftershave. It was spicy and appealing but mingled with the mild aroma of his obviously exhausting day it made for a heady combination.

He reached for the chart as Rose was about to slide it back into the holder, his arm brushing lightly against hers. The action caused shivers to run up her arm and spread throughout her body.

'Uh…' She cleared her throat. 'Excuse me.' With that, Rose turned and walked away. She didn't look back. She didn't pass Go. She didn't collect $200.

What was wrong with her? She asked herself the question over and over again as she climbed into her car and checked the map book. As she started down the road towards her father's house, Rose was determined to get control over her emotions.

She was tired. That had to be it. She'd been under a lot of stress during the past two days and even before that. During the past few months she'd had her break-up with Julian, as well as her decision to get out of Sydney. They were all factors which could contribute to her uncharacteristic behaviour towards her new colleague.

As she pulled into the driveway of her father's double brick house, Rose put all thoughts of her day behind her. Her father had been worried about her driving such a long way by herself, but she'd assured him she would be fine. If he saw otherwise in her expression, it would only cause him to worry and that was the last thing he needed. His wedding day was tomorrow. At last her father had found happiness, and she was glad he'd invited her to share it with him.

'There you are,' Beverley, her father's fiancée, said as she came out the front door and crossed to Rose's side. 'Your father and I were starting to worry.'

'Sorry,' Rose replied. 'There was an emergency. I asked someone at the hospital to call and let you know.'

'They did.' Beverley gave her a warm hug—not a gentle pat on the shoulder but a real hug. A motherly hug. To someone who'd basically grown up without a mother, these hugs were precious. 'I can't believe they've had you working at the hospital already.'

Rose smiled and shrugged. 'What else was I supposed to do?'

'What a welcome to Broken Hill!' Beverley laughed. 'We're so glad you're here.' Beverley hugged her again. 'Come inside out of the heat. We can get your bags later—right now, your father is impatient to see you.'

'How's everything going for tomorrow? All organised?' Rose asked as they walked inside, Beverley's arm linked with hers.

'I certainly hope so. Oh, Rosie, it's so silly. I've been through this before—a wedding, I mean—yet I can't believe how nervous I am.'

'Pre-wedding jitters.' Rose chuckled and patted Beverley's arm, pleased that her stepmother-to-be felt comfortable calling her Rosie. It was a pet name that only the people closest to her used. It showed her that Beverley felt comfortable and relaxed in her presence, and Rose knew this was an important factor for her father.

'Ah, the two most important women in my life,' Reg Partridge crooned as they walked into the kitchen. He took the wok off the stove and walked over to embrace his daughter. 'My beautiful Rose.' He held her possessively for a long moment before placing a kiss on her forehead. 'Your coming is an added blessing upon our marriage. Isn't that right, Bev, darling?' he asked as he held out his arm to his bride-to-be.

Rose felt a lump building in her throat and marvelled at how sentimental she was being. Then again, she hadn't seen her father for a good six months and it had been six months too long.

'I'm sorry I wasn't able to make it home for Christmas,' she told her father.

'I understand,' he said, just like he always did, and she knew he meant it. Reginald Partridge was a unique man, who accepted people for who they were. 'The bonus is that you'll be here for six months and that in itself is a present worth waiting for.' He kissed her forehead again, but when a faint hissing noise sounded, he abruptly let the two women go and rushed back to the stove to remove a lid from a bubbling saucepan.

'What are you cooking? Don't you know what the time is?' she asked, as she sat down at the island bench to watch him. It was a position she'd spent most of her life in— watching her father as he cooked. Now he was about to reap the rewards from another cookbook of his going on the shelves, the photographs having been taken by Beverley.

'I'm making beef in black bean sauce and rice, and there are spring rolls warming in the oven for the entrée. I was going to make special fried rice but we haven't been shopping so I'm missing some of the ingredients.'

'Dad—it's almost midnight.'

'I thought you might be hungry,' he said with a shrug. 'Besides, I was worried about you and you know how cooking helps me relax.'

'Never mind.' She laughed. 'It sounds and smells delicious.'

'I can't believe my good fortune, marrying a man who

likes to cook.' Beverley chuckled as she crossed to his side and kissed him.

Rose watched them and sighed with happiness. Seeing her father like this was one huge weight off her mind. He was happy—at last—and he deserved all the happiness in the world.

If only she could find such happiness, but at the moment she wasn't sure. Broken hearts took a long time to fix or, at least, she assumed this one would. A vision of Dave swam before her eyes and her heart jolted. Her uncharacteristic reaction to the man had completely thrown her, and at the moment she wasn't sure whether it was a good or bad thing.

CHAPTER TWO

THE reception was well under way when a deep voice drawled from behind her, 'What's this? The groom's daughter standing all alone in the corner?'

Even though she'd only heard that voice a few times, Rose knew immediately who it belonged to without turning around. Besides, the hairs on the back of her neck were standing on end and a wave of goose bumps had pricked their way down her arms.

'I'm watching my father and his bride,' she retorted icily, straightening her back even further. 'Not that it's any of your business.' She continued to watch her father lead Beverley around the dance floor, their arms entwined around each other.

'So true.'

'I don't recall seeing your name on the guest list.'

'It wasn't.'

'Do you always gatecrash weddings?'

'Only when there's an emergency.'

Rose turned to look at him then. It was a mistake. She hadn't realised he was *that* close. She breathed in deeply and was treated to the heady combination of spicy after-shave mingled with sweat. It must still be hot outside. 'I…er…thought there was an anaesthetist here to cover the weekend.'

'There *was*. That's the emergency.'

Rose sighed heavily. 'Isn't there anyone else? I don't officially start at the hospital until Monday.' She was cross and annoyed and it helped to dampen her other unwanted feelings. 'This is my *father's* wedding!'

'Aw, come on, Rosie,' he teased, and she widened her

gaze in surprise before bristling at the use of her nickname. 'It won't be a long operation and you know it's better if you do it rather than anyone else. Besides, your old man will be leaving soon anyway.'

'Please, don't—'

She was interrupted by the sound of the band finishing their song and people clapping.

'Ladies and gentlemen,' the MC announced, 'the bride and groom are about to depart.'

'See?' Dave said softly from behind her.

Rose looked away, becoming even more frustrated with the man. She didn't want to miss the opportunity of saying goodbye to her father and new stepmother. It would also give her an excuse to escape Dave's company.

'If you'll excuse me,' she said politely between gritted teeth, 'I'd like to go and say goodbye to my father and Beverley.'

'No need,' Dave replied, and pointed. Sure enough, her father and his blushing bride were headed straight for them.

'Dave,' her father said with delight, and heartily shook the other man's hand. 'Glad you made it after all.'

'Sorry, Reg. I'm here under false pretences. I've come to whisk your daughter away.'

Reg laughed. 'Should I ask whether your intentions are honourable?' her father joked.

'Dad!' Rose couldn't believe it. Her father was actually friends with this man?

'Only joking, Rosie.' Reg leaned over and hugged his daughter. 'I know it's probably an emergency if Dave's come to get you. He wasn't able to make it to the wedding because he was on call.' Reg turned his attention back to Dave. 'I thought you had an anaesthetist for the weekend.'

'We did. That's what I was explaining to Rosie. The locum anaesthetist *is* the emergency. Appendicitis.'

Reg chuckled. 'Always the way. Off you go, then, darling.' Reg embraced his daughter. 'Bev and I are leaving anyway.'

Rose stared, dumbfounded, at her father. It appeared he was throwing her to the wolves, or at least one of them.

'Never mind,' Beverley whispered in her ear as the two women hugged. 'Things will settle down in a week or two. Just take each day as it comes and remember that your father and I both love you.'

It was the exact thing Rose needed to hear. Beverley always seemed to know the right thing to say and Rose was immensely glad her father had married her. He needed a wife and although Rose thought she was too old to need a mother, Beverley had proved her wrong yet again. It didn't matter how old you were, it was still nice to hear that you were loved.

'Thanks,' Rose whispered back.

'Now, have you got the house keys?' Beverley fussed. 'And can you remember the controls for the air-conditioner?'

'I'll be fine,' Rose promised. 'Go. Have a good time and I'll see you in a month's time.'

'Take care of my girl.' Reg shook Dave's hand once more before kissing Rose on the cheek. 'I love you, my darling Rose.'

'I love you, too, Dad.'

'We'd better be going,' Dave said, as Reg and Beverley moved away.

'Oh, she can't go yet,' Beverley protested. 'I almost forgot. I have to throw the bouquet.'

Rose laughed uncomfortably. 'Beverley, that's an out-dated romantic tradition.'

'Well, I'm an outdated romantic traditionalist, then,' her stepmother replied good-naturedly. 'Come on,' she announced to the room. 'I need all the unmarried women in a group.'

'That's your cue, Rosie.' Dave's deep voice said from behind her, as he gave her a gentle shove.

'Don't push me,' she retorted.

'Well, hurry it up, will you? We have an appendix that's ready to perforate and you're standing there like a statue.'

'We'll do the garter toss and the bouquet at the same time,' the MC announced. 'All unmarried women over here and all unmarried men over there.'

The room was galvanised into action and soon the MC was counting to three. With both her father and Beverley standing with their backs to their respective groups, they tossed on the count of three.

Rose realised the flowers were heading for her face and instinctively put her hands up to protect herself, her fingers automatically curling around the handle of the bouquet.

Everyone clapped and cheered and then the wolf-whistling started. She turned to see what all the commotion was about and came face to face with Dave, her step-mother's garter dangling from his index finger.

Dave raised his eyebrows suggestively, which made the crowd laugh even harder. 'If you'll excuse us,' he said, and, placing his arm about her shoulders, led her out of the room. She tried not to focus on the warmth of his touch or the way her body seemed to spring instantly to life. The laughter drowned out any protests Rose might have made, but she just didn't have the energy. Besides, she felt completely and utterly humiliated and embarrassed.

'There you are, Rosie. Safely whisked away from a wedding reception.' He scanned the parking lot. 'Would you like me to unlock your car?'

'I'm more than capable,' Rose retorted. She pulled the keys from her small purse and opened the Jaguar's door.

'All right, then. I'll meet you at the hospital.'

Rose climbed behind the wheel, watching him walk away. He had nice long strides. Sure and determined—just like the rest of him. She shook her head and started the engine, glad of the reprieve from prying eyes. She drove behind Dave's ute towards the hospital, happy to follow him as otherwise she probably would have needed to stop and check the map book.

The whole day had been exhausting and she hadn't needed that extra bit of attention at the end to cap it off. Still, her dad and Beverley had enjoyed themselves and would soon be on their way to Sydney on a chartered flight. Tomorrow, they would fly to Port Douglas in Far North Queensland where they would spend four glorious, relaxing weeks by the sea. That was the one thing her father had confessed he missed the most, living in Broken Hill—the sea.

Rose refocused her thoughts into professional mode as she pulled into the hospital car park. She climbed from the car in her strapless dress of burgundy silk which Beverley had chosen for her to wear as bridesmaid.

'Let's get going, Rosie,' Dave called as he headed into the hospital. Rose bristled once again, frowning as she walked after him. Now was not the time for a conversation on her name. He was right, they had a patient to deal with and they'd already wasted more than enough time.

'Status?' Dave asked the nurse who met them at the door.

'BP is up and he's complaining of more pain.'

'What's he been given so far?' Rose enquired as they continued to walk towards Pre-op.

The nurse rattled off the list of medication and Rose mentally went through what she'd probably use.

'Go get changed, Rosie, while I check on Jim.' Dave continued walking down the corridor, effectively dismissing her.

Rose knew he was right but it was the way he'd done it—speaking to her as though she were an intolerable intern. Once she was dressed, she would go see Jim and have a chat with him before anaesthetising him. While she was doing that, Dave had time to get changed and scrubbed. She was still fuming inwardly at his dictatorial attitude as she headed towards Pre-op. As soon as she arrived, Dave gave her an update, being very specific about how long he thought the surgery might take so she knew how long to anaesthetise the patient for.

'Hello, Jim,' she said, as she looked down at the man lying on the barouche with his eyes closed. 'I'm Rose Partridge.'

'Just get on with it,' Jim growled without opening his eyes. 'I know the procedure so yadda, yadda, yadda, just do it, will ya?'

It appeared Jim wasn't too happy with the turn of events. 'Certainly,' Rose replied as she checked his chart for the vital information she'd need in order to anaesthetise him correctly. She asked him the standard set of questions which he answered in clipped tones before telling her exactly what type of drugs she should use and asking whether she wanted him to do it himself as she seemed to be taking all day about it! Rose kept her cool, knowing it was a combination of agitation, nerves and the pethidine he'd already been given.

Once Dave arrived in Theatre, everything progressed smoothly. Again, Rose was impressed with his skill. An appendicectomy was a routine operation but he performed it with such ease, always monitoring in case things went wrong. A few minutes after the small organ had been removed, it burst with little prompting inside the kidney dish.

'Perfect timing,' Dave announced to his theatre staff. His blue gaze settled on Rose briefly and she noted a twinkle in his eyes. 'Just as well you didn't take any longer to catch that bouquet at the wedding, Rosie.'

'Oh, tell us about it,' one of the nurses asked as Dave once again checked the area for any sign of leakage from the appendix.

Rose glared at him, cross that he'd brought up her personal life within the bounds of Theatre. He raised his eyebrows slightly before turning his attention back to his work.

Rose had never liked mixing business with pleasure, yet here he was doing just that. At her old hospital, she'd kept herself to herself, associating with her colleagues in a businesslike and professional manner. They didn't socialise together, they worked together—and as far as she was concerned, never the twain should meet. She didn't agree with personal relationships with colleagues as she'd seen it cause all sorts of problems.

And then there had been Julian, a small voice reminded her. Well, he hadn't been a medical professional and even though she'd met him while he'd been working at the hospital, it wasn't really the same thing.

Her friends had been gathered from her outside interests and although one or two of them might have known medical colleagues of hers, they respected her wishes and kept the two aspects of her life separate.

Now here was Dave, not only telling the staff about the events at her father's wedding but calling her Rosie in front of them, to boot! They *really* needed to talk—and soon.

Dave directed her to reverse the anaesthetic and headed off to write up his notes. Once Rose was satisfied with Jim's recovery status, she left him in the capable hands of the nurses and headed back to the change rooms. She hoped that Dave was still around as she wanted to have that chat with him.

She went back to Recovery, not sure where he might be. The nurses there thought he might have gone to the ward but instead of sending Rose on a wild-goose chase, trying to find him, they called down to the ward only to be told that he wasn't there.

'He's turned your head already, hasn't he?' one of the nurses said with a nod. 'He's a looker, that Dave. Why, if I wasn't wedded to my childhood sweetheart, I'd be giving the single females in this town a run for their money.'

'No, she's not Dave's type,' the other nurse, who was probably old enough to be Dave's mother, replied.

'Oh, Sadie,' the first nurse remarked. 'How do you know what Dave's type is or isn't?'

'She's a blonde,' Sadie replied, and Rose bristled at being talked about rather than talked to. 'And Dave doesn't go for blondes, even if she does look good in a posh dress.'

'He does so go for blondes. His wife was a blonde—wasn't she?'

'That's *why* he doesn't go for them, and she was a city slicker just like Rosie here.'

Rose was about to ask whether she needed to be here for the conversation, but the mention of Dave's wife intrigued her. So he'd been married. Was he divorced? Had his wife died? Rose wasn't sure why she found the information intriguing and in some ways she resented being told that she wasn't his type—not that she wanted to be—just that she thought, as the man was all grown up, perhaps he could decide for himself who was or wasn't his type.

'He told us how you caught Beverley's bouquet,' the first nurse continued, looking directly at Rose this time. 'And how he caught the garter. How romantic.'

.'Ha! Nothing remotely romantic about young Dave,' Sadie snorted. 'He probably just did that to hurry things up. He knew he had to get back here as soon as possible.' She turned to look at Rose. 'He's not answering so I'd say he's gone home. You should do the same.'

'Ah…all right. Please, call me if you have any problems with Jim tonight, although,' Rose added as they all looked across to where he was snoring peacefully, 'I doubt it.'

As she walked out of the hospital, the heat hit her once more. Did it ever cool off in this town? She dug her keys out of her bag and headed over to where she'd parked her car. It was then she realised there was a dark silhouette leaning against it, and for one heart-stopping second she faltered. She should have asked a security guard to walk her out—then she remembered that she hadn't seen a security guard.

'It's just me.' Dave's deep voice was instantly recognisable and she shivered, not sure whether it was from fright or nervous anticipation. 'Sorry, I didn't mean to frighten you.'

Rose continued towards him, trying desperately to ignore the sudden racing of her heart. 'Is there a problem?'

'No.'

Rose stopped not far from him, now able to see him more clearly due to the lights that surrounded the car park. She couldn't get through to the driver's door because of the six feet four inches of solid male that was blocking her way. Again, she caught the scent of him and clenched her jaw. This had to stop. She didn't even know this man, let alone like him.

'Then would you mind moving, please?' She kept her tone polite and impersonal, not able to bring her gaze up to meet his but focusing on the sun-kissed skin of his upper chest that peeked out from beneath his partially unbuttoned shirt. It would have been safer to look at his eyes, she realised, and did just that.

'I sensed,' he began as he shoved his hands deep into the pockets of his shorts, 'that you wanted to talk to me.'

'And we couldn't do that inside the hospital?'

'I also sensed that you wanted privacy.'

'Then try sensing that I'm extremely tired and would like to go home.'

'Rosie.'

'Don't call me that,' she snapped. She ran her fingers through her hair. 'Sorry. It's just that the last few days have been extremely exhausting and I'm very tired.'

'Why don't you like being called Rosie?' He frowned, staying where he was. 'It suits you.'

'Whether it suits me or not is completely irrelevant. The fact that I'm not used to colleagues of mine calling me by a pet name is reason enough for you to stop it.'

He continued to frown but she saw his lips twitch. 'Actually, I don't know of any pets who are called Rosie.'

'David! Stop teasing.' She was exhausted and she didn't have time for this.

'David? Only my mother called me David,' he added with a laugh. 'It's so…formal.'

'Well, only my father calls me Rosie, which I classify as being informal.'

'Bev calls you Rosie, too.'

'That's different. She's now a member of my family.'

'Well, I'm practically that.'

'Pardon?'

'I did catch the garter after all.'

Despite her tiredness, Rose felt a smile tug at her lips. Instead, she looked down at the ground and made an attempt to push past him. Big mistake. He didn't move. She found herself pressed up against a firm, solid, male chest, his huge hands coming up to touch her arms lightly.

'We've got to stop meeting like this,' he murmured. Before she knew what was happening, he'd bent his head and brushed his lips across hers.

It was only the briefest of touches but it left her feeling breathless and desperately wanting more. Her heart was pounding furiously against her chest and the headache that had taken hold the second she'd pulled out into the Sydney traffic a few days ago vanished into thin air.

'Goodnight, Rosie,' he whispered, and in the next instant he walked away.

Rose forced herself to move. To go through the motions of getting into her car and driving back to her father's house—the house she'd be calling home for the next six months.

What had happened back there? The question was buzzing around in her mind and as she could feel the headache starting to return, she decided it wasn't worth thinking about. Dave—oh, goodness, she didn't even know his last name! Dave, with the softest lips she'd ever felt pressed against hers, could just get out of her head!

Four hours later as she tossed and turned in the unfamiliar bed, she realised it was easier said than done.

Dave wandered out onto the verandah that surrounded the old weatherboard home and stared out at the night sky. Stars twinkled down at him, making him wonder what on earth he was doing up at this hour. It was just past two o'clock and, try as he might, he'd been unable to get to sleep. And he knew why.

Rosie Partridge.

Why had he kissed her? Although it had only been fleeting, why on earth had he succumbed to the temptation and pressed his lips to hers? Sure, she was an attractive woman, but she wasn't his type.

He shook his head, trying for the umpteenth time to clear the vision of Rosie from his mind.

'Just give up, mate,' he mumbled to himself as he sat down in an old chair and stretched his legs out in front of him. Tomorrow—or, more correctly, today—was Sunday and he'd promised his brother he would help with the northern boundary fencing. That's where he'd been on Friday evening, when that horrible accident had occurred. He'd heard the crash and had all but flown to the ute where he'd driven like a madman to the scene of the accident. There, he'd found a vision in white, rendering first aid. At first, he'd thought he'd been seeing things—an angel, dressed in white? In the middle of nowhere? Instead, he'd encountered a woman as prickly as an echidna.

Dave rubbed his fingers around the back of his neck and closed his eyes. The scent of her perfume seemed to be embedded deep within his mind and she'd been here for less than forty-eight hours. How was he going to work alongside her for the next six months and keep his hands to himself?

Then he rationalised that he'd always been attracted to women who were supposedly inaccessible. That had been the initial attraction towards Mags. She'd hated that nickname and he'd used it almost constantly near the end of their disastrous marriage.

Now it appeared Rosie didn't like the nickname he used for her either. Ah…he could pick 'em, all right. The ones who looked great on the outside but weren't too pretty on the inside. Although, in Rosie's case, he wasn't too sure about that.

Dave rested his head against the wall of the house and crossed his arms over his chest. He'd thought he'd out-grown those hormonal tendencies that had him doing things he wouldn't ordinarily do—like going to Reg's wedding to pick Rosie up. Anyone could have gone but he had quickly volunteered to be the gofer and he knew why. He'd wanted to see how she'd looked all dressed up and he hadn't been disappointed with the result.

Sitting there with his eyes closed, he decided to give up fighting the inevitable and allowed different images of Rosie to drift in and out of his mind. The way she walked, with a calm confidence. The way her hips swished ever so slightly, her arms swinging loosely by her side. The way she slowly lifted her chin to meet his gaze and the way her blue eyes had looked after he'd kissed her.

He groaned in exasperation but didn't push the images away. He was only thinking about her—surely that couldn't do any harm. He was the type of man to always learn from past mistakes so there was no way he'd ever need to worry about a long-term relationship with a woman like Rosie Partridge because it simply wasn't going to hap-pen. She wasn't his type and that was all there was to it.

Yet—he'd kissed her.

He'd felt his heart leap at the wonderment and surprise in her eyes but her lips had been soft and pliant beneath his. No other woman had made his heart lurch like that before and it was a feeling he wasn't sure he wanted re-peated. He was divorced—with a child! He had responsi-bilities and they had nothing to do with Rosie Partridge.

There had to be something wrong with him. Perhaps he

was coming down with something or maybe it was due to the busy days he was putting in. Not only was he working at the hospital but he was also helping Mick out with the fencing which was in a bad state and desperately needed replacing.

He allowed his thoughts to wander even more and the next thing he knew, he felt a hand on his shoulder, shaking him awake.

'What are you doing, sleeping out here?' Mick asked, a small grin on his lips.

Dave stood and stretched. 'Just getting some fresh air. What's the time?'

'Six.'

Before his brother could quiz him further, Dave moved into the house, heading directly for the shower. When he was finished, he went to the kitchen to satisfy his growling stomach.

'How long will you be at the hospital, Dave?' Mick asked a few minutes later as he poured his brother a cup of coffee and handed it to him. Dave was just finishing his breakfast and was glad of the refill.

'Hopefully, not too long. I should be back around ten.'

Mick nodded but didn't say anything else. Dave glanced up at him, sensing there was something more. 'Spit it out.'

Mick shrugged. 'Just curious as to why you couldn't sleep last night.'

'Why?'

'Because the last time you couldn't sleep and spent the night on the verandah was not long after you separated from Mags. Is everything all right? Is Mel all right?'

Glad to have the topic off himself, Dave nodded. 'I spoke to her yesterday and she sounded fine but, then, she's six, Mick. How are six-year-olds supposed to sound?'

Mick shrugged. 'So if Mel's all right, why couldn't you sleep?'

Dave groaned and sipped his coffee. 'I just couldn't. It's

been exhausting lately. Doing my work at the hospital and then helping you out—not that I'm complaining,' he added quickly. 'I'm more than happy to help out around the farm, but I'm a doctor, Mick, and a surgeon at that.' Dave put his coffee down and held up his hands, a grin on his face. 'I need to look after these babies.'

Mick's smile increased and he nodded. 'Oh, yeah. It's a woman, all right. So who is she?'

'What? I just told you why I couldn't sleep.'

'It's that new doc, isn't it? Ah, what's-her-name. You know, Reg's daughter.'

'Rosie.' Even the way Dave said her name out loud sounded as though he were a love-struck teenager.

'That's it.' Mick was grinning from ear to ear. 'Woo-hoo. Big brother's going down for the count yet again.'

'Cut it out,' Dave warned, laughter still lighting his eyes.

'Well, if you're not interested, why don't you let me take a crack at her?'

'No way.' His words were vehement but he forced himself to relax. 'Besides, you've already got a girlfriend.'

'So?'

'Mick!' His brother knew how he felt about infidelity.

'Easy on, mate. I'm only having a lend of you. It's just she looked so gorgeous at the wedding and smiled so sweetly at me that I don't know if I'll be able to resist.' Mick's tone indicated he was teasing but Dave felt a tightening in his gut.

'Keep your distance.' Dave pointed his finger at his brother. 'She's not your type.'

'And I suppose she's yours?' Mick laughed. 'Just wait till I tell—'

'Don't you breathe a word of this to anyone,' Dave interrupted, his mirth instantly gone. 'Promise me, Mick. Besides, there's nothing really to gossip about. Understand?'

'Hey, you know I was only foolin' around.' He crossed his heart, the way they had when they'd been kids. 'You

have my word,' Mick promised as he headed for the door.
Before pushing open the screen door, he turned and added,
'For the moment.'

'Get out of here,' Dave growled, and sipped at his coffee. And you, he told himself sternly, get a hold of yourself. If he didn't, soon the whole town would be gossiping.

CHAPTER THREE

ROSE woke up late on Sunday morning, finally having given in to her body's need to sleep. She was glad the spare room, where she was sleeping, had its own *en suite*, complete with a bath. Her room also had a separate entry and exit. That way, when her father and Beverley returned from their honeymoon, she wouldn't wake them if she came in late from the hospital.

She wandered through to the kitchen in search of food and a hot cup of coffee. To her disgust, she only found a piece of stale bread and instant coffee. Ugh. She needed to get all of her things unpacked. Even so, she hadn't bothered to pack any special coffee because she'd presumed her father would have some. Amazingly, for someone who was a chef, her father's kitchen was basically bare. Then again, both he and Beverley had had other things on their mind than doing the grocery shopping before they'd left for their honeymoon.

Rose shuffled back to her bedroom and decided on a shower, especially as it seemed she needed to go to the shops. She took her time beneath the spray, enjoying the luxury of not rushing. That's the way her life had been for the past eighteen years since she'd started med school. Always rushing here or there. Lectures, exams, clinical sessions, operations. If it hadn't been one thing, it had been another. Now she was here she intended to relax a little.

The hospital was a whole seven-minute drive away from her father's house—rather than a forty-minute drive through peak-hour traffic, as the hospital she'd worked at in Sydney had been.

Here, in dusty, hot Broken Hill, she could relax. She

took a deep breath as though to prove it to herself and closed her eyes beneath the warm spray.

Then a vision of Dave appeared in her mind, making her tense. 'No. Relax,' she said firmly. 'Let the thoughts flow.' It was what a psychologist friend had told her before she'd left. Letting the thoughts flow would help her accept the break-up with Julian more easily. Repressing was bad. So why couldn't that work for Dave as well?

She took another breath and let the thoughts flow. He was very good-looking—tall, too. She liked tall men. Julian hadn't been as tall as Dave, she was sure of that. Last night, when Dave had brushed that brief kiss across her lips, he'd had to bend a lot further and her head had been at a different angle.

The feather-light touch of that kiss still seemed to burn on her lips and she raised her fingers to her mouth, expecting to find them hot—but they weren't. She opened her eyes and looked at the shower wall. How could one tiny kiss have such an incredible effect on her? Julian certainly hadn't affected her in this way and they'd been engaged!

'Men!' Would she ever understand them? She turned the taps off and focused her thoughts on something more practical, like what food she needed to buy. She dressed quickly and headed out to her car. It had been parked in the driveway as her father's car was in the garage, and the heat was stifling. She started the engine to get the air-conditioner working while she checked the local map Beverley had left for her, marked with places to eat, where the shopping centres were and some interesting sculptures she might want to see. Broken Hill supported a great artistic community, with outback painters capturing their own interpretation of nature's delights.

Rose glanced at the car clock and was surprised to find it was almost midday. Her stomach growled, making its sentiments known. 'Lunch, or rather brunch first, I think,' she remarked as she checked the map again, deciding on a location at which to eat.

When she pulled into the car park, she realised the place Beverley had marked was nothing more than a pub. An outback pub, she thought as she climbed from the car, her sunglasses still shielding her eyes. The food must be good—after all, her father's tastebuds were quite finicky. Determined to persevere, Rose walked up to the door, automatically swatting flies as she went.

The first thing that hit her as she walked in was the smell of beer, and stale beer at that. The second was the cool breeze from the air-conditioner. The third was the noise. It was as though the place were filled with rowdy school-children, such was the volume level. Rose frowned as her gaze adjusted to the artificial lighting.

She scanned the room, seeing big sweaty men, dressed in some sort of sports uniform, teasing and laughing with each other. Then she spotted Dave. Her lips burned again with the memory of the way he'd made her feel last night, and she shook her thoughts clear. She should have known he'd be the type of larikin to be involved in something as noisy as this. He was sitting on a chair, his elbow up on a table, his palm open in challenge. Seconds later, a victim, who had a shock of red hair, was found and mirrored Dave's position.

'Three, two, one—go!' someone shouted, and the wild cheering began again. Rose stood, mesmerised by the sight of Dave's bulging biceps and his stern concentration as the ridiculous and uncivilised contest continued. Slowly, she lifted her sunglasses from her eyes and held them loosely in her hand, now openly staring at the men and their antics. Dave was putting up a good fight and almost had his opponent's arm down.

Rose's sunglasses slipped from her fingers, bringing her back to reality. Shaking her head at being drawn under his spell, she sighed heavily and bent to pick them up.

Hoots of laughter had her straightening quickly and

glancing over at the table. Dave's blue gaze scorched right through her and for a moment she felt like a roo trapped in the headlights of an oncoming car. She held her breath before looking away.

'How could you lose?' one of the men wailed. 'You never lose.'

She risked a surreptitious glance at Dave, only to see him smiling good-naturedly at his friends as they teased him mercilessly. Dave had lost? Apparently so. She smiled to herself as she headed to the bar, glad that he wasn't so perfect.

Dave watched as Rose sat down on a bar stool. Never had he lost an arm wrestling match to a more stunning distraction. She was dressed in a flowing summer dress, the same reddish-orange colour of Uluru, which buttoned up the front and had revealed a good portion of her long legs when she'd bent to retrieve the sunglasses. It had been those long legs which had cost him his concentration.

'Dave?'

At the sound of Mick's voice, Dave quickly turned his attention back to his brother.

'Yeah?'

'Bit distracted, eh, mate?' his brother asked, his eyebrows raised suggestively. 'And I can see why.' Mick's voice was low but Dave still glared at him.

'Who is *that*?' one of the blokes asked, angling his head in Rose's direction.

Mick ruffled his friend's shock of red hair. 'She's too sophisticated for you, mate.'

'Hey. I like socistifated women,' the bloke retorted.

'Yeah, right,' one of the others chided. 'You can't even say the word right.'

'So who is she?'

'Reg Partridge's daughter.' Dave cleared his throat and looked away. 'She's the new anaesthetist at the hospital.'

'Take me in for surgery, mate. If I get to lie on that

operating table and gaze up at her, I'd be a happy man,' one of them said.

'Yeah—before she knocks you unconscious with the drugs,' Dave added. There was a round of hearty laughter.

'Dave always gets the good-lookin' ones. Mags was a definite looker,' another bloke added.

'Who slept with any bloke she met,' Mick added in defence of his brother.

'Rose is just my colleague.' Dave took a sip of his soft drink.

'Besides, she's a city slicker,' Mick stated, and some of the men nodded. In the outback, the locals stuck together, always polite but never getting too close to those who came and went with the seasons.

'How long is she here for, Dave?'

'Six months.' Dave finished off his drink. 'Well, it was a great practice game today,' he praised as he stood. 'But I've gotta get going.'

'What? You're not staying for lunch?'

'Not today.'

'But, Dave…'

'Ah, leave him,' Mick said as he slapped his brother heartily on the shoulder. 'He was up helping me with the fencing this morning before our hockey game, and he's had a few emergencies in the last few days.' Mick lowered his voice and spoke in a stage whisper. 'Besides, he's getting old now. Almost forty.'

The guys all laughed and Dave grinned at them. 'Two more years,' he told his friends. 'I need to get to the hospital and check on Bob again.'

'When are you gonna let us come and see him?'

'Maybe tomorrow.'

'Everything all right, Dave?' Mick asked, concerned.

'I'm not sure.' Dave glanced over at Rose as he spoke. She was sitting up at the bar, studying the menu. He really should mention that he might be taking Bob back to Theatre. 'I just need to check on him again. I'll see you guys later.' With that, Dave headed over to where Rose sat at the bar, trying to block out the whistles and taunts from his mates.

'Hi,' he said quietly as he leaned on the bar.

'Hello.'

He saw her nose twitch and realised he probably smelt like a wombat. He took a small step to the side, away from her. 'Can I have your mobile phone number?'

'Why?' She turned to look at him, a suspicious glint in her eyes.

'Because I'm heading to the hospital to check on Bob.' At the mention of their patient, the suspicion left her gaze. 'When I saw him this morning, he still wasn't right. One of the drains might be blocked.'

'You want to take him back to Theatre?'

'Possibility. I wanted to let you know.'

'I appreciate it.' She turned her attention back to the menu. 'I'd better decide what to order, then.'

'The hamburger is good,' he offered. 'Unlike those fast-food restaurants, this hamburger is healthy. Or, if you want something light, try their breakfast omelette. It's delicious.'

'Thanks.' When he didn't move she looked at him again. 'Something else?'

'Your mobile number?'

'The hospital has it.'

Dave pulled his mobile phone from his shorts pocket. 'I'd like it just the same. In case I need to call you away from the hospital.'

The thought of the brief kiss they'd shared jumped into her head. 'W-why?' she asked, clearing her throat, cross with herself for stuttering.

'In case there's an emergency and I'm not at the hospital,' he stated matter-of-factly.

'Oh.' She felt foolish and switched her anger towards him. How dared he make her feel this way? She rattled off her number and watched him programme it into his phone before the bartender came up to take her order.

'I'll have the fish, thank you,' she stated.

'Don't make it too big a serve,' Dave butted in. 'I might need her in Theatre soon.'

'Right you are, Dave,' was the man's reply, and Rose felt like knocking both of their heads together. Arrogant pigs.

Rose was determined to put him in his place. She might be physically attracted to him, she might have to work with him, but she didn't have to bow to his every whim. 'Was that all you wanted, Dr...?' She stopped. He'd done it again. Because she didn't know his last name, she wasn't able to put him in his place.

'What? Is there something wrong?' Dave stared at her with concern.

'No. Go see your patient and leave me to eat as much of my lunch as I have time to.' When in doubt, go for the direct dismissal. She was proud of herself for regrouping and after a few heart-stopping seconds, when she thought Dave was going to say something else, he finally turned and left her in peace, waving to his friends as he went.

She was halfway through her lunch, grudgingly acknowledging that Dave had been right to suggest a small-ish portion because she was almost full, when she realised someone was standing beside her.

'G'day. I'm Mick. We met at the wedding yesterday.'

Rose forced a smile. She'd met so many people yesterday and she knew she wouldn't remember them all.

'Thought I'd give you some time to eat before coming to say g'day. Dave said he might need you at the hospital.'

'Yes,' Rose replied as she forked in another mouthful of the delicious steamed fish fillet.

Another man joined him—the one with the red hair who'd been arm-wrestling with Dave. 'G'day. I just wanted to say thanks for walking in when ya did.'

Rose frowned at him. 'What do you mean?'

'You distracted Dave.' He laughed. 'He was so busy ogling you that I managed to beat him at arm-wrestling.' He shook his head in bemusement. 'First time for everything.'

Rose wasn't quite sure how to receive this information. Surely that wasn't the way it had happened, was it? Had Dave been ogling her? She knew he must find her attractive at least, otherwise how could she explain that brief kiss last night?

So Dave had been ogling her! A small surge of feminine power shot through her but she focused her attention on the men before her.

'So, what do you gentlemen do for a living?'

'I'm a pastoralist, mainly cattle,' Mick replied. 'And this bloke is my best stockman.' He clapped his friend on the shoulder.

'And how long have you lived in Broken Hill?'

'All our lives. Dave and I were born here but our old man got work in Melbourne and a couple of other places so we moved around a bit.'

'Dave?' Rose frowned as she looked at Mick.

'Yeah. He's my brother.'

Now she could see the family resemblance. Their colouring was the same—both with dark hair, although Mick's was a bit longer than his brother's and had started to curl at the ends. Also, Mick's eyes were brown, whereas Dave's were as blue as the night sky. 'I see.' Rose put her knife and fork together on the plate, unable to finish her lunch. 'So how long since you came back to Broken Hill?'

'Ah…let's see.' Mick looked down at his hands, concentrating. 'Dave moved back here after his marriage broke up, which was about six years ago, and then I came not long after that so, yeah, about five, six years.'

Rose nodded slowly as she digested this information. He was divorced! Then that *definitely* meant he wasn't her type because she wasn't interested in divorced men. From her limited experience, they often had too much extra baggage, and if there were children involved—well, it just made matters worse. She didn't need that type of aggravation in her life. Especially as Julian had supplied her with enough aggravation to recover from.

'Food too much for you?' Mick smiled. It wasn't as engaging as his brother's and didn't make her heart race.

'Yes. Delicious, though.' Her mobile phone shrilled to life. 'That will probably be your brother,' she told him as she reached into her bag and pulled out the phone. 'Dr Partridge,' she said automatically.

'I do need you, Rosie,' Dave's deep voice said down the line, and Rose felt goose bumps spread over her skin. For one fleeting moment she imagined he was saying those words in a different context, but thankfully she came to her senses.

'I'll be right there,' she replied, and before he could say anything else, she disconnected the call.

'So I take it Bob needs further surgery?' Mick asked.

'It looks that way.' Rose collected her bag and slid from the stool before taking out her purse to pay for her meal.

'Uh, allow me.' Mick pulled his wallet from his shorts.

'No, really. It's fine,' Rose insisted.

'I'd let him if I were you,' his mate added. 'Mick and Dave have got a strong sense of um…what's it called again? You know, that knight in shining armour thing?'

'Chivalry,' Mick supplied. 'It's called chivalry, mate.'

'Yeah, that's it.'

Rose decided she could spend more time here arguing with the two men than it would take her to drive to the hospital. Conceding was the only way out. 'Well, thank you very much. I appreciate it.'

'My pleasure.' Mick's smile had a glint of teasing in it and Rose wondered whether there wasn't something going on here that she didn't know about.

She headed for the door and was surprised when the rest of the men Dave had been with called goodbye to her. She smiled shyly and waved before almost bolting through the door into the heat.

She was still smiling when she walked into the hospital.

'You look…happy,' Dave remarked as he met her in the corridor.

'Thank you. And why shouldn't I be? Your brother just bought me lunch.'

'He *what*!'

The smile vanished and Rose frowned at Dave's attitude. 'He bought me lunch. Insisted on it.'

'I can imagine,' Dave grumbled.

'What's the matter?' Rose eyed him suspiciously. 'Is there some sort of bet or something going on that I don't know about?'

'Bet? No. Just Mick being Mick.' He clenched his jaw tightly.

'Well, he was very charming.'

'He has a steady girlfriend.' Dave's voice was low and held a hint of warning. 'In fact, I wouldn't be at all surprised if they announced their engagement soon.' It was stretching the truth a little but Rosie didn't know that.

'Good for them,' Rose said without concern. 'What's that got to do with me?'

'Don't go getting any ideas on making moves on my baby brother, Rosie.'

She took offence at that. 'I never said I was going to.'

'He's not equipped to handle women like you.'

'I beg your pardon! What's that supposed to mean?' Rose stopped outside the female changing rooms and glared at him. She was pleased to see he looked apologetic and watched as he raked an unsteady hand through his hair.

'That didn't come out right. Just that you're, you know, a city slicker.'

'I'm a what?' Her voice was calm and controlled and he knew he was digging himself in deeper.

'A city slicker.'

'How would you know? You know nothing about me, David…' Oh, how she wished she knew his last name. That way, when she told him off, it would carry more clout. It was starting to drive her insane but there was no way in the world she'd ask. She had too much pride to ask him that *now*.

'So, are you trying to tell me that you're not from Sydney? I read your résumé,' he continued. He knew her credentials. Where she'd trained, what papers she'd written. That she was thirty-six and had never been married— but that was about it. It had said nothing about the way her smile could light up a room or that when her eyes were flaming with temper, as they were now, she looked vibrant.

'I came *here* from Sydney but that doesn't mean I'm a city slicker. So, before you start sticking labels on me, I suggest you check your facts first.' With that, she turned and walked into the female changing rooms, glad he couldn't follow her.

She went to the locker she'd been assigned and wrenched it open, muttering to herself.

'I'll have you know…' Dave's voice boomed as he followed her.

Rose jumped in fright. 'What are you doing in here?'

'I'm talking to you. I'll have you know it's considered rude to walk away from someone when you're having a discussion.'

'We're not having a discussion,' she all but yelled at him. 'You're in the female changing rooms and I want to get changed for surgery, or do I need to remind you that you have a patient waiting for your expert attention?'

'Don't you remind me of my responsibilities, girly.'

'Don't you "girly" me. My name is Rose. Not chick, bird, sheila or any other names men around here call women. Rose. R-O-S-E.'

Dave looked at her. 'Finished?'

Rose lifted her chin in defiance. 'For now.' At least her

temper was cooling but, ooh, that man could get her hot under the collar.

'Right. Let's get to Theatre and we can finish this discussion later.' He paused before adding, '*Rosie.*' There was a smirk on his face as he left her alone.

Rose was so infuriated that for the first time in her life she wanted to throw something at someone. She scowled as she went through the motions of getting changed. She didn't understand him. Not one little bit. First he was happy, then boiling mad and in the next instant he was as cool as a cucumber. Men!

She counted to ten and then, deciding that wasn't enough, counted to twenty, before leaving the changing rooms and heading to Pre-op. Bob was obviously still in pain and after Rose had spoken to him and read his chart to find out what analgesics he'd already had, she gave him a pre-med. They transported him to Theatre and started getting things set up. Dave walked in once Bob was anaesthetised and the operation began.

After an hour, Dave was ready to close, satisfied that his patient shouldn't have any further complications. He'd mentioned that the orthopaedic surgeon, Penny Hatfield, would be in Broken Hill the following morning and that Rose's services would be needed.

It was just after five o'clock when Rose headed out to her car, feeling exhausted. She frowned as she unlocked the door and climbed in, not exactly sure why she was feeling so tired.

'Probably the heat,' she mused as she started the engine and pulled out of the hospital car park. When she arrived home, she ran a warm bubble bath and sank gratefully into the tub. She rested her head back and closed her eyes.

A startling pain in her abdomen woke her up. The water was cool and her fingers were wrinkly, indicating she'd been in the water for quite some time. Rose shifted and shivered as the water moved against her skin. She sat up

and started to get out of the bath, only to find that the
muscles in her arms were weak and lifeless.

Another pain had her closing her eyes and holding her
breath until it passed. She waited a moment before trying
to get out of the bath again and this time was successful.
Rose wrapped herself up in a bathrobe, the effort sapping
most of her energy. After a small rest, she stumbled out
of her bathroom.

She made slow progress and she leant against the wall
for support, unable to believe how shaky and lifeless her
legs were. What was wrong? Obviously something—but
what? Rose slid down the wall onto the floor, glad her legs
no longer needed to support her. Another pain gripped her
and she tensed once more.

She closed her eyes and rested her head on the soft
carpet, letting fatigue claim her.

'Rosie?' The call came from a distance. A place far
away. Rose could hear it but she couldn't do anything
about it. She was trapped. Her arms and legs were made
of lead and there was nothing she could do about it.

'Rosie?' A pounding accompanied the voice and the
next thing she knew she was being scooped up off the floor
and placed on a comfortable bed.

The comfort only lasted for a second as the pain en-
gulfed her. Her arms were wrapped around her waist, her
eyes closed in agony.

'Rosie, here. Swallow these.' She heard the voice and
knew it was one she'd heard before. It wasn't her father.
It wasn't Julian—Julian had never called her Rosie. It was
familiar, one she'd dreamt about. She thought hard.

'You've got food poisoning,' the voice said, and this
time she recognised it as Dave's. Dave was here, taking
care of her. Dave always called her Rosie.

She opened her mouth to speak but nothing came out.
Instead, she concentrated on swallowing the pills, uncaring
what they were. She trusted Dave. He was a doctor. He

wouldn't give her anything bad. Dave always called her Rosie—and she liked it.

Dave sat by her bed, amazed at what she'd just mumbled. She *liked* it when he called her Rosie! Well, there was a turn-up for the books. He smiled to himself, feeling extremely pleased with this bit of information. And here he'd thought she didn't like him.

He stayed with her for the rest of the night, often just content to watch her sleep. She was beautiful. No doubt about that. Even though she was sick with food poisoning, she was still stunning.

He reached out and touched her forehead. She was a lot cooler now and as she'd already had her second dose of paracetamol, he knew she was over the worst. Thank goodness she hadn't been as bad as Mrs McGill, who was in hospital, her body still racked with spasms.

When the first patient had arrived at the hospital, complaining of abdominal pain, the registrar on duty had asked Dave to check her out. Then the second and third had arrived not long after. They'd managed to trace the origin of the contaminated food and had discovered it had been the fish served at the pub that afternoon.

The owner had been horrified. Dave knew he'd leave no stone unturned until he found out who was responsible for selling bad fish to him.

Dave had been in his car, heading to Rose's house, the instant they'd discovered the source. He knew she'd be all alone and his worst fears had been confirmed when he'd let himself into Reg's house, thankfully knowing where the spare key was kept.

His own stomach had lurched in anxiety when he'd seen her collapsed on the floor. He leaned over her bed and breathed in deeply, enjoying the floral scent that had wound itself around her from her bath.

During the past five and a half hours that he'd been there, Dave had helped Rosie to the bathroom and had sponged her forehead until her temperature had broken, as well as ensuring her fluids were maintained.

He'd gone into the kitchen and made himself a cup of tea and some toast, surprised to find that Reg didn't have much in his cupboards. Then again, the man had had other things on his mind. Dave smiled to himself as he remembered how happy Reg had looked on Saturday. With that image came one of Rosie dressed in her bridesmaid outfit, and with that came a tightening in his gut.

He glanced at her, sleeping peacefully. Her hair had dried all funny from lying on the pillow while still damp. Even still, she looked beautiful. Amazing. He was seeing this woman—a woman he'd known for only a few short days—at her worst and she was still beautiful.

It brought back thoughts of the way her body had looked, naked and flushed from the fever. Twice he'd had to change her clothes. The first time had been to get her out of the bathrobe, which hadn't helped in reducing her body temperature, and the second had been after the fever had broken and her body had stopped sweating.

Dave returned to the kitchen and made himself a cup of tea. It was almost two o'clock in the morning. Fatigue from his very long day was settling in and, after returning to Rosie's room, he sat in the chair, stretched his long legs out and let his head rest against the wall. Although her bed was big enough to accommodate both of them, he didn't want to risk raising her body temperature.

The sound of coughing woke him and he sat up, instantly alert but taking a few seconds to figure out where he was. He turned his head and saw Rosie lying in the bed, and memories of the night before returned. He checked the time.

'Eight o'clock!'

The sound of his voice caused her to stir and he quickly reached out a hand to rest it on her forehead. Her temperature was normal.

'Dave?' she whispered brokenly, and he reached for the glass of water with a straw that he'd put by the bed.

'I'm here, Rosie. Have a drink.' He was glad that she was aware of her surroundings. It was a good sign.

'Thank you,' she said, after swallowing a few small mouthfuls.

'How do you feel?'

'Like I've been hit by a Mack truck.'

Dave chuckled and the sound washed over her, warming her insides. 'Glad to hear it. I'm just going to ring the hospital,' he said as he started out of the room. 'I'll be back in a moment.'

Rose lay still and slowly opened her eyes. The few times she'd tried during the night, the room had been spinning on its axis. This time, though, everything seemed to be staying in its proper place.

When Dave came back into the room, she ventured a smile. 'How's everything at the hospital?'

'Settled. Five patients presented to A and E complaining of stomach pains and two of them were admitted with food poisoning.'

'How are they?' Rose asked with concern.

'One is stable, the other lady, Mrs McGill, still has a temperature.'

'Oh, dear.' Rose shifted slightly and groaned.

'What's wrong?' Dave was instantly by her side.

'My muscles ache.'

He smiled sympathetically. 'Normal, I'm afraid.' He sat in the chair. 'You were quite ill at one stage but once that passed you started to pick up.'

'Would you mind helping me to sit up?' she asked, and he was up on his feet again, assisting her. 'Thanks,' she said once she was propped up against the headboard of her four-poster bed.

He was frowning at her

'What?' she asked cautiously.

'You.' He sat on the side of her bed and met her gaze.

'I'd expected you to be…I don't know, indignant at me being here.'

Rose smiled. 'That would be ungrateful and my father raised me with better manners than that. Last night I was sick and I needed someone to take care of me. I never would have been able to cope by myself and I *am* grateful to you for coming.'

'You surprise me.'

'Because most women would feel inferior for showing their weakness?' When he nodded she continued, 'Sickness such as food poisoning isn't being weak, it's being sick. I guess a lot of people don't know the difference.'

Dave smiled, a slow, sexy smile that had her heart beating double time. 'So matter-of-fact. You're not what I expected, Rosie Partridge.' He leaned closer, placing one hand on the bed by her side.

'Is that a good thing?' Was that *her* voice so husky and seductive? She swallowed, the charged moment between them growing with each passing second.

'I'm not sure but I'm willing to find out,' Dave murmured, his lips only a hair's breadth away from her own.

'Are you going to kiss me?' Rose whispered, her gaze flicking down to his lips that were still curved into a slight smile.

'Any problems with that?'

Rose's heart was pounding so fiercely against her ribs she was certain he could hear it. She parted her lips, her breath coming out in a rush. 'Um…' Her tongue traced the contour of her lower lip, wetting it in anticipation. That brief kiss he'd pressed to her lips the other day was still firmly imprinted there. She *wanted* a repeat but…

His nose touched the tip of her own. Dave was going to kiss her. *Really* kiss her, and she wanted it more than anything in the world. As his lips moved in closer she reluctantly lifted her fingers and held them between their mouths.

Dave pulled back slightly, his gaze inquisitive.

'Let me at least brush my teeth first,' she whispered.

CHAPTER FOUR

Rose knew she had to get out of the shower sooner or later. She couldn't hibernate in here for the entire six months of her contract, although that was exactly what she felt like doing. How could she have been so careless as to let things go so far?

Sure, she was grateful that Dave had come to look after her and she really appreciated it, but to let the man almost kiss her? Was she insane? Dave was dangerous and she'd known it from the first moment she'd seen him. Dangerous, at least, to her own equilibrium.

She reluctantly turned the taps off and took her time towelling herself dry. He was waiting for her to finish her shower before he left, to make sure she didn't have any relapses of the cramps or fever.

Rose once more had been grateful as her muscles were still quite weak, but she was feeling better than she had half an hour ago. Half an hour ago when Dave had almost kissed her!

'Keep it light. Keep it professional,' she told her reflection, before pulling on underwear and a cotton summer dress. 'The man is dangerous.' She combed her hair back, glad to be looking more herself. 'Dangerous, and don't you forget that.'

She still remembered the look in his face when she'd asked him to leave the door to the *en suite* open but to close the door to the bedroom. His gaze had skimmed her body quickly, a puzzled frown on his face.

'I'm not good in confined spaces,' she'd added by way of explanation. In fact, it had taken her years to be in a room with a door closed—or in a car without feeling mildly claustrophobic.

He'd nodded, still looking confused, but had acceded to her wishes. She sat on the bed for a few minutes, realising how weak she felt. Just to shower and dress had knocked the stuffing out of her.

Taking a deep breath, she stood and walked to the family room where she thought Dave might be waiting. He wasn't there. She listened for a moment but couldn't hear anything. Had he gone? Perhaps once he'd heard the water stop, he'd left. She felt a momentary sense of loss at the thought and then a flood of relief. If he'd left, then she wouldn't have to worry about facing him right now, especially after that intense moment before she'd stopped the kiss.

Heading into the kitchen to make herself a cup of tea, Rose stopped short in the doorway when she saw him standing with his back to her, looking out the window over the sink. Her stomach contracted, and it had nothing to do with the food poisoning. Her mouth went dry and she instinctively put a hand out to lean on the bench as she felt her knees go weak.

His shoulders were broad beneath the striped cotton shirt he wore. She knew from before that it would be unbuttoned, revealing a white T-shirt that was half tucked into his navy shorts. The front of the T-shirt was snug and defined his torso as though it was moulded to it.

His legs were lean and long, indicating he worked out often, although he didn't strike her as the gym type. She wondered if he helped his brother on the farm. His dark brown hair was ruffled and as his fingers combed through it again, Rose itched to follow the movement with her own hands.

She closed her eyes and shook her head, desperate to control her wayward thoughts. What had got into her? She was behaving very out of character and she knew it was all because of Dave. Dave, whose surname she still didn't know.

'Are you all right?'

At the sound of his voice, Rose opened her eyes, only to find that he'd moved and was standing in front of her, his arm coming out to steady her. Rose forced her legs to support her weight and moved out of his reach.

'I'm fine. Thank you.' She added a smile, realising the words had come out brisk and dismissive.

'You're a liar,' he contradicted. 'I can see perfectly well that you're not up to standing for too long.' He ushered her over to a stool and sat her down. 'Tea? I'm afraid that's about all there is to offer. There's not much in your father's pantry.'

'Oh, that's right,' Rose groaned. 'I was going to get some groceries yesterday after lunch but…' She shrugged, letting her words trail off.

He nodded in understanding. 'Somehow our jobs seem to get in the way of any other plans we might make.' He switched the kettle on and jangled the car keys in his pocket.

Rose took that as a hint that he'd rather leave. 'Don't worry about making me tea,' she said rather briskly. 'I can do it.'

'What about food?'

'I'm really not that hungry but I'll go out later today and get some food.'

'You'll do nothing of the kind,' he counteracted. 'Doctor's orders.'

'But I've got to anaesthetise for the orthopaedic surgeon. I have to go out so I may as well get some groceries while I'm at it.'

'You're not anaesthetising.'

'What? Why not? It's my first official day at work.'

'Not any more.'

'Have you reorganised my schedule for me?' Rose was a little indignant at his high-handed attitude.

'Rosie, you've just had food poisoning.'

'I'll be fine to anaesthetise. It's not as though I'll be standing on my feet, operating. I'll be sitting down, monitoring my dials.'

'The orthopaedic surgeon is bringing her own anaesthetist.'

'And how do you suppose she knew to do that?' she asked rhetorically.

'I called Penny last night and asked her to.'

'Do you always organise everyone at the hospital?'

He grinned, not at all concerned about her censorial attitude. 'Only when they've had food poisoning and are too stubborn to realise they're still not one hundred per cent recovered.'

At his words, Rose glared at him. 'Stubborn? You're calling *me* stubborn?'

'Are you implying that *I'm* stubborn?'

'Absolutely.'

'When?'

'When you came and took over Bob's treatment at the accident site. Oh, no, wait a minute,' she corrected. 'That wasn't stubbornness, that was arrogance.'

'Arrogance?'

'Yes. Now, stubborn—let me see. Ah, yes, when you came to my father's wedding and insisted upon me accompanying you. No, no, wait. That wasn't stubborn either, that was domineering.'

'What?' He stared at her with incredulity.

'How about when you warned me to keep away from Mick? Yes, now, *that* was stubbornness—or was it stupidity?' She sighed heavily. 'Oh, I give up, Dave. I guess you're all those things, and all of those attributes make up the typical Aussie bloke.'

'Well, if I'm a typical Aussie bloke, what does that make you?'

'I'm a sophisticated, modern woman, of course,' she countered quickly.

'Come off it, Rosie. You only think you're sophisticated and modern. I won't quibble with the woman part, though.' He gave her a quick perusal. 'Definitely woman.'

'Do you mind?'

'Mind what?'

'Not leering at me.'

'Oh, so now I'm a leering bloke as well.' A deep chuckle accompanied his words and Rose's skin broke out in goose bumps again. He was doing it again. Affecting her when she didn't want to be affected.

'Don't you need to get to the hospital?'

'No. Why?' He took a step closer to her. 'Are you trying to get rid of me?'

'But you have patients with, ah…food poisoning.'

'No, I don't. The GP who admitted them has patients with food poisoning.'

'Surely you're going to do a ward round. It's Monday morning. All surgeons do rounds first thing Monday morning.'

'I think you'll find things work slightly different here in the outback. I'll go in later today when things aren't so hectic.' He took another step. Rose wanted to turn tail and flee, but knew her body was still too weak. As for anaesthetising, well, she knew she could cope but she also acknowledged that it would knock her out. Dave was right—again—and she didn't like that one bit.

'Rosie? What's wrong? You've gone pale.'

'I'm fine,' she snapped. 'And don't call me Rosie.'

'Why not?'

'Because I asked.'

'But I have it on good authority that you *like* me calling you Rosie.'

'Don't be so silly.' Then she glanced up sharply. 'Whose authority?' she demanded, thinking her father might have said something.

'Yours.'

'Pardon?' Her eyes widened in surprise.

'You. You were talking in your sleep last night and you said that you liked it when I called you Rosie.'

She blushed. There was no way she could control it and she did her best to hide it. Dipping her head, she stared at the ground, trying to figure out how to get herself out of this one. 'I was delirious,' she finally retorted.

Dave closed the distance between them and slowly raised her chin until their eyes could meet. 'Yes,' he said softly. 'You were delirious, but in my experience that's when people's inhibitions are down and the truth comes out.'

Rose felt as though she were burning up inside beneath his close scrutiny. His blue gaze was probing her own, seeking a response that she knew he'd find there. She found him attractive. Immensely attractive. And it was clear that he felt the same way about her. Yet they were so wrong for each other. In fact, surely this morning had confirmed it because all they'd done since she'd walked into the kitchen had been argue.

It now looked as though he was going to follow through on his earlier impulse to kiss her, and to her surprise she realised she wanted it more than anything. There was one thing that was bothering her and as he started to lower his mouth to hers she stopped him once more.

'What is it?' The deep, husky tones washed over her. 'Your teeth look nice and clean now.'

She smiled shyly. 'Um…it's not that. It's…um…your name.'

'Sorry?'

'Your surname,' she amended. 'I don't have any idea what it is.'

'My surname?'

'Yes. Everyone I've met so far calls you Dave! No one seems to use your surname at all. I just thought that as you're about to kiss me, I…you know…might as well ask,' she said with determination.

'Absolutely. Why not?'

'I mean, we haven't really been properly introduced.'

He smiled and nodded. 'You know, you're right.' He looked down into her blue eyes, eyes that were so pretty, that radiated her intelligence and concern. 'Allow me to rectify the situation.'

Leaning closer, he softly cleared his throat. 'Rosie Partridge,' he brushed his lips gently across hers. 'Meet…' another kiss '…Dave Dunbar.'

'It's a pleasure,' she whispered against his mouth.

'Yes, it is,' he reflected, and bent his head, his lips slow and seductive on her own. Rose's head whirled with excitement and she felt her stomach churn with nervous butterflies but delighted in his touch at the same time. She sighed and closed her eyes as his mouth continued its onslaught.

His body shuddered with pleasure at her response and he pressed another gentle kiss on her lips before spreading tiny kisses down her face, around her neck to her ear. Oh, she smelled incredible, all sweet and light, and Dave felt his desire for her triple. How could someone who was so wrong for him feel so right?

And she *was* all wrong for him, he rationalised as he placed one last kiss on her lips before moving away. He'd been burnt once before and he'd vowed never to let it happen to him again. Beautiful, irresistible, gorgeous blonde women were to be avoided at all costs.

Dave watched as she slowly opened her blue eyes which were glazed with longing but held a hint of confusion. 'You need to rest,' he whispered, and then cleared his throat. Taking two huge steps back, putting some distance between them just in case he succumbed to the desire to take her in his arms and kiss her senseless.

The urgency of the emotion surprised him. All the more reason to get out of there—fast. He backed towards the door. 'I'll get someone to bring over some food for you,' he commented. 'If you rest today, you should be fine by tomorrow, but I'll call back later and see how you're doing.'

Rose watched as he continued to back away from her. What had happened? One minute he'd been kissing her and the next he was all but sprinting out. What had she done to turn him off? She bit her lip. 'You don't need to come by. I'm sure I'll be fine.' Her voice was cool and dismissive. He'd obviously found something inadequate about her and was desperate to leave. Julian had been the same, except he'd been quite open and brutal about her inadequacies, telling her to her face that she'd never make a good wife.

'I'll still come by and check,' he said firmly.

It was just the doctor in him, she told herself when her hopes started to rise again. She squashed them back into place, forcing herself to deal with the facts. He evidently regretted kissing her just now and she wanted him out of the house as fast as he apparently wanted to run.

'Well, as you let yourself in, you can let yourself out. I'll see you later, then.' She would have loved to have stood and walked away but wasn't at all sure her body would respond to her brain's signals.

'Right, then. See you later.' He stared at her for a second, his jaw clenching. In the next instant, he was gone. She listened as the back door opened and then closed with a final thud.

Rose sat there for a while, unable to move even if she'd wanted to. She balled her hands into fists, determined not to cry, but it was devastating to know that although men found her attractive, they also found something lacking in her.

It was obvious from the way Dave had retreated after those kisses that he felt the same way towards her as Julian had. Julian, who she'd thought she would end up marrying. After all, wasn't that what people expected when they became engaged?

Slowly and on wobbly legs, Rose made it back to her

bedroom and collapsed on the bed, tears rolling silently down her cheeks before she fell into a restless sleep.

When Rose went to work the next day, she wore her most professional suit, determined to keep the relationship between Dave and herself strictly business. As it turned out, she didn't see him at all. Or the next day, or the next.

She'd been grateful to Mrs Fredrick, her neighbour, who'd brought over some groceries on Monday and had stayed for a brief chat, mainly talking about her father's wedding and how wonderful it had been. Rose hadn't remembered meeting Mrs Fredrick but, then, she'd met a lot of people that day.

Dave's elective operating list alternated between Thursdays and Fridays, and this week Rose had to wait until Friday to see him. It was the first time since Monday evening, when he'd dropped in for a whole two minutes to check on her, that Rose was able to take another look at the man who had haunted her dreams since her arrival in Broken Hill.

'Feeling better, Rosie?' Dave asked as he walked onto the ward before the start of his theatre list.

'Much, thank you,' she replied lightly, and that was the extent of the personal conversation between them. On his list that morning was a five-year-old boy called Joe who had intestinal cysts that required removal. Rose and Dave went to see him together.

'Dr Rosie here is going to give you some medicine that will make you very sleepy, and when you're having a great dream, I'll fix your tummy up so you don't have any more pain.'

'Will I dreaming about swimming in the sea?' Joe asked, his eyes alive with excitement.

'Absolutely,' Dave replied, and looked at Rosie. 'Make sure you give Joe some sleepy medicine that has dreams about swimming in the sea.'

Rose raised her eyebrows but smiled politely at the boy and nodded. 'Of course.'

'Then, while you're splashing about in your dream, I'll take the sick piece of your tummy away and make sure the good bits are working real beaut. How's that sound?'

'And then I won't have a sore tummy any more?'

'Well, it will be sore for about a week or two, but after that you'll be back to your old self again.'

'Yay.' Joe clapped.

'Now, Dr Rosie just needs to check you out before giving you some special medicine.' Dave ruffled the boy's hair before stepping away, a smile lighting his face.

Rose's own smile was pasted on as she manoeuvred around to do Joe's observations. 'Poke your tongue out for me,' she said, shining the torch down his throat and pressing his tongue with a depressor. 'Say "ah".'

Joe complied and gagged a little. 'Everything looks fine,' she said, before wrapping the blood-pressure cuff around his arm. She pumped it up and listened with the stethoscope. Joe was talking to her but she needed to listen and concentrate. 'Just a minute,' she said. When she was finished, she looked at him. 'What was your question?'

'What's that thing called?'

'A sphygmomanometer.' She continued with her observations, just wanting to get it over and done with as soon as possible. She gave him a pre-med, telling him how good he was before quickly heading back to the nurses' station, sighing with relief.

'That's a big sigh,' Dave said from behind her. He leaned forward onto the counter and handed Rose Joe's case notes. 'Looking for these?'

'Yes. I just want to make some notes in them.'

'Cute kid, eh?'

'Hmm? Oh, Joe. Sure.'

'Problem?'

'No. Kids and I just don't mix, that's all. I feel...' she shrugged '...totally uncomfortable around them.'

'You don't like kids!' Dave was shocked.

'What?' Rose asked defensively. 'You look like a stunned mullet. What's so wrong with that?'

'Uh…uh…nothing.' She'd taken him completely by surprise. 'All you need to do is relax and be honest with them. They're not that difficult to deal with.'

'I haven't had a lot of contact with kids,' she replied matter-of-factly. 'Not even when I *was* a kid.'

'Why?'

'Kind of personal, don't you think? Besides, you've got a theatre list to start or we'll be running late all day.' Rose closed the case notes and slapped them up against his chest before she walked off. She was starting to shake and didn't need the third degree from Dave. Now was not the time to be dredging up old memories. She had patients to focus on.

Joe's surgery was completed without complication and Dave didn't speak to her unless it was absolutely necessary.

For the next two weeks, things didn't change. Rose's life, professionally, was great. She'd had two postcards from her father, saying that he and Beverley were having a wonderful time. The people in Broken Hill were welcoming and friendly but she still felt like an outsider. She guessed the locals saw her as a city slicker and that was that.

The following Monday, Rose was just coming out of Theatre, after anaesthetising for Penny Hatfield, the orthopaedic specialist from Adelaide, when Carrie, one of the theatre nurses, rushed up to her.

'Dave needs you in A and E, stat.'

Rose followed and was taken to the doctors' tearoom. There were several people there, all sitting down listening to Dave as he spoke.

'The Royal Flying Doctor Service will take us out to the airstrip on the property and then someone will meet us there and take us to the accident site.' He turned his head, his gaze encompassing Rose. For a split second she saw a flicker of pleasure but it was so quickly veiled that she wondered if she'd imagined it. 'Two teenagers are trapped. There appears to have been a subsidence on their property. Possibly an abandoned mine. It may still be unstable so I want everyone to exercise the utmost care.'

'Injuries?' Rose asked, her tone completely businesslike.

'Full report isn't in as no one's been able to get to them. We'll be the first medical team on the scene. Rosie—get what you'll need then come back here. You and I will head out to the airstrip together so you don't get lost. Everyone else, you've done this before, you know what to do. Let's get moving.'

Rose stood paralysed for a moment as others around her started leaving the room, talking about what they needed to do. She'd known when she'd taken this job that she might need to travel in a small aircraft, but she hadn't expected it to be this soon. The fear started to grip her heart, just as it had always done when she'd had to get on a plane—big or small.

'Something wrong, Rosie?' Dave asked, noticing she wasn't moving.

'Plane? You said we're going in a plane? H-how big is it?'

'A nine-seater. Why?'

Rose swallowed over the lump in her throat and wiped her clammy hands on her skirt. 'Ah…nothing.'

The room was now empty, except for the two of them. Dave peered at her closely before raking a hand through his hair. 'You don't like to fly, do you?'

'Not particularly,' she admitted.

'It was part of the job description. You knew you'd be flying in a light aircraft.' His tone was anything but sympathetic. In fact, he seemed rather annoyed and, truthfully, she couldn't blame him.

'I know,' she snapped, her fear being replaced by anger.

'I just hadn't expected it to be so soon.' She took a deep breath. 'I'll be fine.'

'You'd better be.' With that, he turned and headed out of the room.

Rose remained where she was, trying to control the churning in her stomach and the prickling in her eyes. Well, what had she expected? For him to say it would be all right and to hold her hand? She was a grown woman. She'd been working on her mild claustrophobia for years and had improved dramatically, but could she *really* do this?

There were no questions about it. She *had* to do this.

Straightening her shoulders, she went to get her equipment ready, forcing the overwhelming memories of the past back where they belonged. She was a professional. She could do this.

She returned to the tearoom a few minutes before Dave arrived, but it was enough to make her palms start perspiring again.

'Ready?' he asked, his tone tough.

'Yes.' Rose knew he was questioning her and she raised her chin defiantly, not wanting him to get the better of her. There were people out there, people who needed their expert help, and above all she couldn't allow herself to lose sight of that.

'Let's go.'

They headed out to the car park and climbed into Dave's ute, ever careful of her medical bag with the drugs she would need to help alleviate their patients' pain.

'So why are you afraid to fly?'

'I'm not afraid,' she countered quickly.

'No? Your body language says otherwise.'

'And tell me, Dr Freud, what does my body language tell you? Other than I'm anxious for our patients.'

'Is that why every muscle in your body is tense? Look, Rosie, I was only trying to help.'

'I don't need your help.'

'Why are you so antagonistic towards me?'

'Why shouldn't I be? Ever since I arrived in this town, all you've done is badger and pick on me.'

'Pick on *you*? You've been as prickly as an echidna. You city slickers—you're all alike. You come here, we try to make you feel welcome, perhaps ask a few questions to get to know you better, and suddenly we're being accused of badgering. Well, I'll have you know that I've never ''badgered'' in my life and I don't intend to start.'

'Ha. I doubt you even know what the word means.'

'It means to harass or nag.' Dave turned off the road into the RFDS car park. 'Only women nag,' he muttered as he parked.

'What?' Rose asked in disbelief. 'That's just the sort of sexist comment I'd expect from you,' she added as she climbed from the car, medical bag in tow. If she'd known where she was going, she'd have stormed off ahead of him. Instead, she had to cool her heels whilst he got out and collected his gear. 'What makes you think that the word ''nag'' is related only to females?'

'Because every female I know nags,' he said firmly, as he stalked ahead of her.

'Well, every male I know badgers.'

He stopped and turned to face her. 'Then I guess we're just going to agree to disagree. The only reason I asked the question in the first place was because I thought I might be able to help you, but I see it was just another wasted effort.'

'What do mean, *another*?'

'Forget it.' He continued on his way, bursting through the reception area of the building before heading out the back. 'You're just spoiling for a fight. Well, you can pick on someone else, Rosie. I won't be your whipping boy.'

'My *what*?' She noticed the strange looks from the rest of the staff who'd gathered there, but she didn't care. She was too mad with him to notice anything at the moment. 'How dare you even imply that any of this was my fault?

You definitely started this argument and then you walk away. What kind of man are you?' They were walking across the hot tarmac, heading towards the plane.

'The kind who really can't be bothered with this at the moment. Stay inside your cocoon, Miss High and Mighty. See if I care.' She watched him climb the small steps and disappear into the plane.

'There you go again. Throwing out blanket statements and then disappearing before you can be confronted with the truth,' she called out, as she mounted the steps and went after him.

Only the two of them were on the plane at that moment, and once she was inside she put her bag on the floor and turned to glare at him. It wasn't as easy as it should have been as the roof was so low that both of them had to crouch down. It was then she realised what he'd done.

She felt the blood drain from her body and her limbs start to shake. 'It's OK, Rosie. It's OK,' he said softly, as he placed his hands on her shoulders. He sat her down in a chair and looked into her eyes. 'You'll be fine. Just keep a clear head and you'll do fine.'

'I'm…I'm…' She felt her stomach clench with nervousness. Her eyes were wild with fear and her head started spinning. 'I'm on a…' Her breathing was becoming more rapid as the seconds passed.

'Breathe,' Dave instructed. 'You got this far, you can do the rest with ease.'

'I'm…I'm…'

The look of panic in her eyes had Dave cursing himself for being so uncivilised towards her, but he'd had to do something to get her onto the plane. He'd hoped their argument could have lasted a little longer—like until they'd touched down—but Rosie had become aware of her surroundings only moments after stepping onto the aircraft. Now she was hyperventilating.

He reached for a paper bag and held it over her mouth

and nose. 'Breathe,' he instructed calmly. 'Let me strap you in. Close your eyes. It'll be fine.'

'It…it won't,' she stammered, shaking her head.

Dave took her hand in his and squeezed it tight. His gaze met hers and his eyes seemed to hold her captive. 'It'll be fine,' he said again. 'I promise. Trust me, Rosie.'

It was what her father had said to her when she'd been a little girl, waking in the middle of the night after one of her horrible dreams. Thanks to the neuroses her mother had left her with, she felt doomed to deal with this mild claustrophobia for the rest of her life. But she was stronger than that and she refused to succumb to it.

'You'll be fine, Rosie,' he said again. 'Trust me.'

She nodded slightly, amazed at how he'd helped her to calm down. Slowly her breathing started to return to normal.

'Nice and calm. That's it.'

The other seven members of the medical retrieval team were starting to board and Rose kept her gaze fixed on Dave's. He monitored her during take-off, holding her hand until they landed. Even then, he undid her seat belt and helped her from the plane, giving her one of his dazzling smiles that turned her insides to mush.

'You did great,' he said softly, before calling his team to order. 'All right, everyone. Listen up.' Dave gave out instructions to the team, letting them know that once they had both patients retrieved and were ready to return to Broken Hill, there would be limited room in the King Air B200C. 'With two stretchers, we'll only have room for myself, Penny, Carrie and Rosie. All right, everyone knows their job so let's get going.'

There were two utes waiting for them at the airstrip and everyone clambered in. 'How're you doing now?' Dave yelled as he crouched down next to Rose in the back of the vehicle. The noise of the tyres on the dirt road was deafening. She was glad they were in the first ute as the tyres were also kicking up at lot of dust, almost obscuring the second ute from their vision.

'Better. Thanks. I've never travelled in a ute like this, but I guess it's the only way to transport everyone and the equipment to the site.'

'Too right,' he said with a chuckle. 'Let the wind blow through your hair—even though it's slightly longer than mine.' He laughed again and Rose smiled at him, thankful that they were out in the open again. She took a few deep breaths, knowing she had to relax and regroup so she could be of use to the patients.

'Probably best if you close your mouth, too.'

'Pardon?'

'If you're going to practise deep breathing,' he said close to her ear, 'close your mouth or you'll either get dust, bugs or both in there.'

Rose's eyes widened in surprise but she quickly closed her mouth. Dave laughed again at her reaction. As they bumped along, his arm kept brushing hers and she enjoyed the spark of excitement that spread through her every time they touched.

The land around them was almost devoid of vegetation and the orangey-brown dirt seemed to stretch on for miles. It seemed arid and depressing, although she was sure other people here would have a different view. She looked at the faces of those around her. Penny was laughing with Carric, who was sitting beside her. The two women seemed oblivious to their surroundings or the amount of dust that was settling over them.

As she looked out again, she saw some emus in the distance. She'd never seen an emu in the wild before—only in a zoo. It was an amazing sight which made her smile. Perhaps it wasn't so depressing after all.

Finally the ute slowed down and went over a cattle grid, the jarring bumps making her teeth chatter. She looked around at her colleagues again. No one was talking now.

Everyone seemed to be concentrating on what they might find, running through different scenarios in their minds.

Once the ute stopped, Dave helped Rose out, the brief touch of his hands about her waist warming her insides. She swatted the flies away. 'Thanks.'

'No problem.' He turned and helped both Penny and Carrie as well, and she remembered his brother's remark about chivalry. People were bustling with activity, the constant swatting of flies making it almost look comical. Rose was able to focus firmly on her work, until Dave walked over with an abseiling harness for her.

'What's that for?'

'For you to put on.'

'Why? I don't need to go down there.'

He nodded. 'Yes, you do.'

Rose felt her heartbeat increase again at the thought of going down beneath the ground. She'd been out on retrievals before but they had all been inner-city accidents. None of this out in the back of beyond and down a hole! How on earth, after everything she'd been through so far, was she going to tell Dave that she couldn't do it? He already had a harness on, as did Penny.

He held up the harness—a piece of woven nylon which was supposed to support her weight as she hung on a rope. Was he mad?

When she looked up at him, she knew her face was as pale as before. 'I take it you've never abseiled before.'

Rose shook her head, unable to speak.

'Let me help you into the harness, then.'

'What? You're not mad with me?' Her words came out rather breathlessly and she watched him eye her carefully.

'Put one leg through here,' he commanded, but didn't answer her question. 'If these harnesses aren't put on correctly, we're all in trouble,' he added, knowing she'd probably be able to complete the task herself but he *wanted* to help. He *wanted* an excuse to be this close to her again.

Dave could tell she was agitated and wasn't sure

whether it was from the thought of abseiling or going into a confined space again. Probably the latter.

When Rose placed her hand on his shoulder to help herself balance, his restraint nearly broke. He should have assigned someone else the job of helping her into a harness but he hadn't been able to bear the thought of any other man getting that close to her.

There were two other females on the retrieval team but they were both busy. The past two weeks of agony, as he'd kept his distance from her, was making him forget his resolve not to touch her again. Not in a personal sense, anyway.

As he pulled the harness up her legs, he felt her hands cover his own. Thinking she wanted him to back off, he tried to pull away. She didn't move her hands.

'Rosie?' He glanced at her, only to see anguish and fear present in her eyes once more. He was beginning to realise there was a lot more to this woman than he'd originally thought. She seemed deep and complex. He knew he should probably turn and walk away but he couldn't help himself. He guessed it was his inbuilt sense of chivalry that made him want to help. That—or his attraction for her was definitely leading him astray.

'Rosie?' He swallowed over the dryness in his throat as he spoke her name again.

She opened her mouth to speak but found she couldn't. Instead, she shook her head. All he could think of was pressing his lips to hers but the fear in her eyes stopped him. She needed reassurance and although he thought that was a fantastic way to reassure someone, she might not be of the same opinion.

'You'll be fine,' he continued, his tone soft and reassuring. 'I'll go first, which means I'll be down on the bottom, helping to control your descent. Unfortunately, the hole is too narrow for both of us to go down side by side, but you'll be fine. Trust me.'

'I do,' she whispered. 'But it's not only the abseiling. It's the…the…'

'The confines of the hole? It'll be all right. Those kids need you, Rosie. Focus on them and how much you can help them. That's why you became a doctor in the first place—to help people. They need pain relief and you're the only one who can figure out exactly what they need. I'm counting on you. We're all counting on you and I know you'll come through for me, just like you did for the plane ride.'

He continued to secure the harness and reluctantly removed his hands from beneath hers. They were standing so close that if he'd just leaned down slightly, he'd be able to claim her lips with his. He was aching to do it but the last thing she needed now was to be frightened further, and he knew for a fact that the kiss he wanted to give her would be anything but reassuring and gentle. He wanted to plunder her mouth with his, which made his earlier chivalry seem like a lie.

The thought of kissing her caused him to lose sight of everything but his growing need for the woman before him. He knew how she tasted and the knowledge had driven him insane for the past couple of weeks. Rosie Partridge seemed to be one woman who refused to leave his dreams, so in the end he'd given up trying to force her out. At least that way he got some sleep, even if he did wake up frustrated.

'Rosie,' he murmured, his voice deep with desire. He edged forward so their noses were almost touching.

'Dave?' Penny called out, and he immediately stepped away from Rose. 'We're almost set.'

'Be right there,' he called back. He glanced at Rose. 'Time to get you roped up. Come with me.' His tone was brisk, mainly because he was cross with himself for almost kissing her in front of the hospital staff. He headed off towards the others, leaving Rose to follow behind him. When she was there, he called everyone to attention.

'Those two kids down there need us. Let's focus on what we're here to do, people, and let's get those kids out in one piece.'

As he continued giving instructions, Rose smiled at what he'd said, feeling some of his inner strength spread throughout her. He was a good man, a good leader, and she *did* trust him.

'Ready?' he asked, turning to face her.

She nodded, concentrating her thoughts on the two teenage kids. They hadn't asked to be down there. It wasn't their fault. They needed her help and she was determined to give it to them.

'Yes,' she said weakly, but cleared her throat and tried again. 'Yes.' It was firmer this time. Dave placed his arm on her shoulder and squeezed it gently.

'Trust me, Rosie. I won't let you down.'

He gazed down into her eyes and she realised he wasn't just talking about the retrieval.

CHAPTER FIVE

THE entire time Rose was abseiling down into the dark hole, caving helmet with a light secured firmly to her head, all she concentrated on was the sound of Dave's voice. He was constantly encouraging her, telling her it was only a little bit further, and before she knew it, she stretched her foot and felt the ground beneath her.

She sagged with relief.

'Well done. Right,' Dave said into his walkie-talkie. 'Send Penny down next and then the stretcher.' He turned to look at her, keeping the light from his helmet out of her eyes. 'Unhook your rope, like I showed you, then come carefully this way,' he instructed. He shuffled to the left and as Rose turned her head to survey the cavern, she was surprised to find it bigger than she'd expected.

'Quite large, isn't it?'

'Yes.'

He knelt down beside their patients who were both currently unconscious. 'That's why I told everyone to clear the area above us. The last thing we need is another cave-in.'

Rose shuddered at his words.

'Don't think about it. We'll be fine.'

There it was again. That reassuring tone she was coming to know so well.

'I've done a quick check. Shenae, who is fourteen, has fractured both her legs and possibly her pelvis. It looks as though she was first down.'

'You know these people?' Rose asked in amazement.

'Of course. This part of the country may be large in area, but as far as the population goes we're actually quite

76

small. Her brother, Ian, is sixteen, and it looks as though he might have fallen on top of her when he came down, which is why I'm concerned about her pelvis. Penny will probably want to take both of them back to Adelaide with her but let's get them stabilised first.'

'Right.' Rose checked Shenae's pulse and blood pressure before roughly calculating her height and weight. Dave was doing the rest of the observations, constantly calling to both patients, hoping they'd soon regain consciousness.

'I don't like Shenae's blood pressure,' Dave said. 'If her pelvis is fractured, like I suspect, then she could have a multitude of internal injuries.'

'I'll put an IV line in and start the saline going.'

'Good.' They worked well together and with the arrival of Penny, the small cavern started to feel crowded. Rose forced herself to relax and concentrate on the patients.

'You know what they say,' Penny joked. 'Three's a crowd.' She laughed but her hands were busy the entire time, feeling bones and making diagnoses. 'Shenae's pelvis doesn't feel too good.'

Rose watched as Penny looked at Dave. They exchanged a glance that was full of meaning. Rose had seen it before—a concerned look often passed between surgeons who were worried about their patients. It made her wonder how long Penny and Dave had been working together. She knew Penny lived in Adelaide and only came to Broken Hill once a week for an orthopaedic clinic and operating session, but there seemed to be...something more between them. She'd noted that Penny didn't wear any rings on her fingers but, then, she'd only seen Penny in Theatre prior to this. She wondered whether the pretty orthopaedic surgeon had designs on Dave. Rose felt her stomach twist and it had nothing to do with the confines of the space they were in.

Rose had finished inserting the IV lines in both patients, and shortly after she'd done Ian's he started to moan.

'Ian?' Dave called. 'It's Dave. Everything's going to be all right, mate.'

'Ow.' Ian continued to moan and Rose didn't blame him. The poor kid had been through the wringer.

'Take it easy,' Dave continued. 'We're going to give you something for the pain.' He nodded at Rose who took her cue. She drew up an injection of morphine and administered it. Ian's face relaxed within seconds.

'He's fractured his left femur, left tib and fib,' Penny rattled off. 'Right tib and fib and I don't like the look of his right olecranon. Does he need anything else, Rose, or will the morphine be enough for me to straighten out that elbow?'

'He should be fine.'

'Ian?' Penny said, and explained what she was about to do. Rose had used Ian's left arm for the IV, noting that the right elbow was at an odd angle. Thank goodness Penny had still been around when this call had come in.

Once Ian's elbow was back in a more normal position, Rose and Penny manoeuvred him onto the stretcher and secured him with the straps. He'd need to be taken out vertically but the stretchers were well equipped to hold the patient firmly so he didn't sustain further injuries in the process.

'Ready to move,' Penny said into the walkie-talkie, after Dave had quickly checked the ropes and knots. 'I've only done this sort of thing a few times,' Penny confided to Rose. 'Dave here seems to do it all the time.'

Dave was now crouching back by Shenae's side. 'Part of being an outback surgeon,' he replied. 'Penny, I'm not at all happy with Shenae's situation.' All three of them crowded around the patient. 'Her blood pressure still isn't good, despite the saline.'

'Open?' Penny asked.

'I think so.'

'Midazolam,' Rose responded, and administered the short-acting sedative. She hooked a stethoscope on so she could monitor Shenae's heartbeat. Without all of her usual equipment, Rose knew she was going to have to do things the old-fashioned way.

Penny and Dave prepared Shenae for an abdominal incision. They'd pulled on sterile surgical attire and draped Shenae as best they could.

'I'm just going to find the offending artery and suture it off,' Dave mumbled from beneath his mask. 'Then we'll get her out of here. If we don't…' He raised his head, his gaze meeting Rose's. She knew what he'd been about to say. They all did. This young girl was not in a good state. 'Ready, Rosie?'

'Ready,' she replied, and watched as Dave made a neat incision into Shenae's abdomen. Rose concentrated hard on her job for the duration of the operation. The seconds passed, ticking into minutes. Five minutes, ten minutes.

'That's the one,' Dave said as he and Penny worked closely together. Due to the lack of light, it had taken longer than normal but, still, they'd found it. 'All right. Let's close her up and get a dressing on this wound so we can get out of here. How's she doing, Rosie?'

Rose performed the neurological and neurovascular obs. 'Picking up nicely.'

'That's what I want to hear,' he mumbled as he concentrated on what he was doing. 'Rosie always tells me what I want to hear.' His tone was laced with humour and right now all three of them could use some.

'Is that so?' Penny queried with interest, her eyes gleaming with laughter as she glanced at Rose.

'Absolutely,' Rose agreed. 'I say things like, "Patient is anaesthetised, Doctor," and, "Patient is stabilised."'

Penny laughed. 'Those are the types of words I like to hear from my anaesthetists as well.'

'Must be a surgeon thing, then,' Rose said and Dave's rich laughter filled the cavern.

As they continued preparing Shenae for the stretcher, Rose decided grudgingly that she liked Penny. So what if the other woman was interested in Dave? Dave was nothing to Rose—except a colleague. She glanced at him and felt her stomach twist into knots again. A colleague she found attractive, she amended honestly.

They waited until Shenae had been transferred to the surface before a rope ladder was hung over the opening of the hole and lowered down to them.

Some dirt and small rocks tumbled down the hole as well and Rose gasped in fright, flattening herself against the wall. 'It's all right, Rosie,' Dave crooned as he quickly went to her side. He placed his arm around her shoulder, but as more small rocks and dirt started to fall, she buried her head into his shoulder, knocking her helmet off.

Dave grabbed the walkie-talkie with his free hand. 'What's going on?' he asked.

No response.

He waited before calling again. 'Keep away from the opening.'

More rocks started to come down and they were getting bigger. Dave pulled himself away from Rose as he helped Penny finish packing up their equipment. Rose whimpered but couldn't move. The tears, the fears—they were all starting to threaten her resolve. She could hear Dave's muffled tones as he spoke on the walkie-talkie but she couldn't listen any more.

She shut her eyes and put her fingers in her ears, trying to block out the loud pounding noise, and only belatedly realised it was her own heartbeat. The smell of the dirt filled her nostrils. Tears streamed down her cheeks as she drew her legs even closer to her chest, her body trembling with fear.

'Rosie?' Dave's arms were back around her, holding her. Cradling her. His hand stroked her hair, comforting. The sobs started to rack her body, her breath coming in gasps.

'Paper bag?' he said to Penny. 'She's hyperventilating.'

'Claustrophobia?' Penny queried as she searched

through the medical kits. 'I've got sutures, IV lines, saline, drugs, but no paper bag!'

Dave processed this information before turning his attention to Rose. 'Rosie? Sweetheart? You need to take some deep breaths. Come on, you can do it.' Dave demonstrated by taking deep breaths himself. 'You need to slow it down.' He felt Rose move beneath his arms. 'That's it, sweetheart, and another one. Nice and big. That's right. Keep going.'

Rose blocked out everything—everything except the sound of Dave's voice and the strength of his arms securely around her.

'Fantastic. You're doing a fantastic job.' He kissed the top of her head as she took another deep breath. She slowly lifted her head to look at him, her frightened blue eyes telling him how hard this was for her to do. 'And another. That's it.' He brushed his lips across hers. 'You did it. You did it.'

Rose heaved a heavy sigh and collapsed against him. 'Penny, see how the opening looks now,' he instructed. 'We need to get Rosie out of here.'

'It's stopped.'

'Check the ladder.'

'Feels strong.'

Dave spoke into the walkie-talkie. 'How's things up there now?'

'Stabilised.'

'Beauty. Rosie's coming up.'

'No.' Rose shook her head.

'Yes, sweetheart.' Dave bent and helped her over to the opening, placing her helmet back on her head. 'You can do it. The sooner you get out, the better you're going to feel. Just concentrate on where you're putting your feet and your hands on the ladder. That's what you need to focus on, Rosie. Can you do that for me?' While he'd been speaking, he'd hooked her abseiling rope back to the D-clamp attached to her harness.

He was nodding encouragingly and she copied it. 'That a girl.' He placed her hands onto the ladder. 'Up you go, Rosie. You've done an incredible job and all you need to do now is carefully climb your way out. Nothing to it,' he said more softly in her ear.

She could feel the warmth of his chest pressing into her back. 'Take a deep breath and let it out, nice and slow. You can do this, Rosie.' Rose was glad he felt so positive because right now she wondered how on earth she was supposed to find the strength to even move, let alone climb a swinging, unstable rope ladder.

She nodded, knowing her vocal cords would definitely fail her should she attempt speech. Doing as he'd said, she took a firm grip on the ladder with both hands and hauled herself up. The slight swaying sensation made her feel ill and for a second all thought was gone. The fears started to swamp her again and she wondered how she would ever get out of this tiny hole when she could barely see the light at the top.

'You can do it, Rosie.' Dave's encouraging words broke through her haze and she forced her body to carry out the instructions her brain was sending. After what seemed like an eternity, she was at the top and being helped up the last bit by two of the rescue party.

'Well done, Doc,' one of the men said.

Rose managed to control her shaking legs until she'd checked on the status of her patients before crumbling to the ground in relief. A few sobs worked their way up and she let them bubble over. She'd done it. It was over. She sat forward and stuck her head between her knees, hoping the light-headedness would pass quickly. She needed to be in control. She had patients to attend to but the feeling that she'd been spun around and shot into space refused to leave her.

She supposed she should be extremely proud of what she'd done. She'd flown in a light aircraft and had been in a very confined space. Part of her wanted to jump for joy at what she'd accomplished but she seriously lacked the energy.

The other part wanted to close her eyes and wake to find it had all been a horrible nightmare but, then, Dave's kisses could never be classified as a nightmare. A dream? A hope? Oh, yes, but never a nightmare. Even though she told herself she didn't really like him, even though they had next to nothing in common, he was a fantastic kisser and she couldn't deny it.

How long she sat there, she wasn't sure. When she raised her head, it was to see Penny climbing out of the hole. Most of the medical equipment had been sent back up and the two patients were being closely monitored by the trained staff.

Slowly, Dave materialised not long after Penny, and Rose watched as the orthopaedic surgeon spoke animatedly with him. She could hear the excitement in Penny's voice but couldn't decipher exactly what she was saying. In the next instant, Penny had flung her arms around Dave's neck and pressed her lips to his.

Rose felt as though she'd been physically hit.

Bile rose in her throat and her head started to spin again. Did Dave go around kissing all the women he worked with? Disgust, not only with him but with herself, came hard on the heels of jealousy. She should have known better. Anyone who kissed as well as he did, who could make a woman forget everything around her, didn't get to be *that* good without a lot of practice.

As Penny disengaged herself from him and headed over to the patients, Dave turned his head and met Rose's gaze across the crowded patch of land. Even though it was now well into the evening, the stars that were out and the half-moon giving them some light, Rose knew his gaze was boring into her soul.

Finally, after long seconds, he broke away. He mumbled something to someone before heading in her direction.

'Hey, how are you feeling?' His voice was soft and

caring, and Rose clenched her jaw, determined not to succumb to his charms any more.

'Fine.'

He stared at her for a moment, his gaze narrowing
slightly at her clipped tone. 'Good. Glad to hear it.' He
reached out a hand to rest it on her forehead but Rose
jerked away from him. 'What's wrong?'

'Nothing.' She stood as though to prove her point, hoping her legs didn't let her down. 'I presume we'll be heading back a.s.a.p.?'

'Uh, yeah.' Dave frowned at her. 'You sure everything's
all right?'

'Fine.' With that, she headed back to the patients.
'Status?' she asked, and received a full report from the
nurses. It was a few seconds before she realised Dave had
followed her and was listening intently to everything that
was being said. Rose was having a hard time controlling
her unwanted emotions towards him. He stood close beside
her and she could feel the warmth emanating from his
body. She was cross with herself for being so aware of
him. It wasn't fair, especially when Penny moved to stand
on the other side of him.

'Something wrong, Rose?' Carrie asked.

Rose was stunned for a moment. 'No. No everything's
fine.'

'You were just frowning so hard at what I was saying
I thought something must be wrong.'

'No. Just tired,' Rose offered quickly. 'It's been a
very…stressful night.'

'Then let's head back to the hospital,' Dave directed.
Each of the utes had a patient in the back tray. 'Rosie and
I will go with Shenae. Penny, you and Carrie go with Ian.'

'Right,' Penny and Carrie replied.

'See you at the airstrip,' Dave called with a wave as he
climbed in the ute next to Shenae. 'Up you get, Rosie.
This part of the journey isn't so bad.'

Rose merely nodded and set about checking Shenae's

vital signs and the saline drip. Once they were on their way and both were satisfied with Shenae's condition, Dave sat down next to the stretcher, resting one arm along the side of the ute.

'You've done such a wonderful job,' he told her.

'Thank you.'

'You sure you're feeling all right? You're acting really weird.'

'Tired,' Rose corrected.

'So do you always speak in monosyllables when you're tired?'

'Yes.'

'I see.' There wasn't much he could say to that and for a while neither of them spoke. Both concentrated on Shenae until they were closer to the airstrip. 'How do you think you'll do, going back in the plane?'

'Fine.'

'Well, if you want to hold my hand or lean on my shoulder, just let me know,' he said with a forced smile.

'Thanks.' Again her tone was clipped and she couldn't look at him when she spoke. She was finding it increasingly difficult to keep up her anger when he was being so darned charming and considerate. He's not your type, he's not your type, she kept repeating to herself.

'Rosie…' The ute came to a gentle stop. 'Take a deep breath and you'll be fine.'

Rose knew it was going to take more than a deep breath to wash away the feelings of his betrayal. It was quite ridiculous when she thought about it. He'd never indicated they were an item or anything special. All he'd done was to kiss her a few times—that was all. Why couldn't she get past this?

'Thanks.'

She concentrated on getting the patients transferred to the plane, ignoring the sickening sensation as she climbed aboard. Knowing she could focus on the patients helped dramatically and that was precisely what she did, never once looking directly into Dave's eyes and only speaking to him when absolutely necessary.

They were all yawning by the time the plane touched down. Penny had decided to send Ian directly back to Adelaide and had called on ahead to make the arrangements. Dave wasn't too happy with Shenae. Although she was holding her own, she would still require immediate surgery.

An ambulance ferried them back to the hospital, and the instant they walked in, Dave started barking orders. 'Blood transfusion, stat. Rose, get her anaesthetised and ready for surgery the instant she's out of Radiology. Penny, come into Theatre with me so we can patch her up before you take her on to Adelaide.'

While she had the chance, Rose went and had a quick shower before getting dressed in theatre garb, hoping she had time for a cup of tea before Shenae was back from having X-rays done.

When she arrived in Theatre, Shenae's condition had improved dramatically because of the blood she'd been receiving. Everyone was ready for Rose to anaesthetise and when Dave walked into Theatre, the scent of him flowed past her, making it difficult to concentrate for a moment.

Rose kept a close eye on her dials, forcing herself not to snatch glimpses of just how well Penny and Dave worked together. How dared he kiss her if he was involved with Penny? Just because Penny had been out of town, did he think he could use anyone as a substitute? No, not anyone—the new girl. The new girl who didn't know about his relationship with Penny. The main factor that stuck in Rose's throat was that, unlike herself, Penny was a brunette.

Stop it, she berated herself. Concentrate.

The operation went well and Dave was happy with the status of Shenae's internal injuries, as was Penny.

'I'll want the pelvic fracture to "rest" for a few days before I decide exactly how I want to approach it. Invasive or non-invasive remains to be seen. Her other fractures are stable and can be fixed back in Adelaide. How soon can I move her, Dave?'

'Give her an hour or two and then she's all yours,' he remarked, as Shenae was wheeled to Recovery. Rose went with her, wanting to stay with her until she either woke from the anaesthetic or was taken to Adelaide.

She stayed by the young girl's bedside until her mother was brought in to see her. Dave came with her, introducing her to Rose.

'Is she going to be all right, Dave?'

'It's not going to be easy, Libby, but at the moment she's definitely holding her own, which is a good sign.'

'But she's…she's…unconscious.'

'It's mainly due to the anaesthetic,' Rose told Libby. 'I'm hoping she'll come around before she's transferred to Adelaide.'

'But all those tubes and things.'

Rose smiled compassionately. 'I guess it does look a little scary but Shenae's doing a good job of recovering on her own. Her body's been through a terrible trauma and right now it needs time to regenerate and recover.'

'What about Ian?' Libby asked, turning her worried gaze to Dave.

'I'll call through to Adelaide and get an update for you.'

'John, my husband,' she said to Rose, 'has flown down there in our little Cessna. He called me when he got there but I haven't heard anything else.'

'I'll get a call through right away,' Dave reassured her, before walking off.

'Can I get you a cup of tea or coffee?' Rose asked, feeling empathy for the distressed mother. Libby didn't answer. Instead, she came closer to Shenae and held her daughter's limp hand.

'I feel so responsible.'

'How could you have known?' Rose asked. 'From what we've learned, no one knew that mine shaft was even on your property. It's been over a hundred and fifty years since people were mining that part of the country. You weren't to know.'

'I know, but I'm their mother. I'm supposed to look out for them. When they were little 'uns, we were always so careful of their outdoor boundaries. We had fences everywhere but now…now they're so…'

'They're so much older and you don't feel you have to watch out for them as much—and they wouldn't let you anyway. From my experience with teenagers, they know *everything* and no one, let alone parents, can tell them any different.'

Libby smiled a watery smile and nodded. 'That's true.'

'They were both taken unawares. It's not your fault, Libby, and you'll do neither Shenae nor Ian any good if you start blaming yourself. They've both been found and they're both going to recover. It won't be easy but once Shenae regains consciousness, we'll have a better idea of how her recovery will progress.'

'I have the update and it's all good news,' Dave said as he returned. 'Ian is still in Theatre but I managed to get through on the phone and Sam, the orthopaedic surgeon who's taken over Ian's care, said that everything is going like clockwork. He'll give the hospital a call once he's finished and let us know what's happening. I spoke to John as well and he said to pass on that he loves you.'

'Oh!' Libby started to cry. Dave didn't hesitate and placed a comforting arm around her shoulders.

'Cry it out, Lib. Cry it out. Your babies are doing fine.'

Rose came around to the other side of the bed to check the readings from the machines once more. 'She's coming around,' she whispered, and, sure enough, a moment or two later Shenae's eyelids started to flutter. Another moment and they were open, staring unseeingly up at the ceiling.

'Hi, there, gorgeous,' Dave crooned.

'Shenae? Shenae?' Libby queried anxiously. 'Mum's here, darling.'

'This is Rosie,' Dave introduced her to Shenae. 'She's just going to check your eyes.'

'I won't be a moment, Shenae,' Rose said softly, as she shone the medical torch briefly into the teenager's eyes. 'Pupils equal and reacting to light, as previous.'

'Mum?' Shenae whispered, but choked on the word.

'Let me give you some ice chips.' Rose quickly spooned a few into Shenae's mouth and when the girl tried to speak again, Dave told her not to worry.

'Rest now. The rest will do you good.'

'They're going to move you soon,' Libby told her. 'We're going to go to Adelaide, which is where Ian and Dad are. We're going to be together as a family and we'll get through this,' Libby told her daughter with determination. 'Ain't gonna be easy but we'll do it.'

'That's the spirit,' Dave said as they all watched Shenae drift off again. The nurses came over to perform their observations while Rose continued to monitor her patient's pain relief. An hour later, they were taken back to the airstrip and, with Penny in tow, Libby and Shenae headed off to Adelaide.

Rose had another shower at the hospital, knowing by the time she made it home, all she'd want to do would be to crawl into bed and sleep the rest of the night away. She forced her legs to work, putting one in front of the other as she walked towards her car.

'So that was Monday,' Dave said as he caught up with her. 'How are you feeling?'

'A lot better, thank you.' Her tone was polite and dismissive.

'I wanted to catch you before you left to say that I'm really proud of what you faced today. It couldn't have been easy.' Dave obviously wasn't taking the hint. Usually her body language and polite tone got the message across to most males. Obviously, Dave wasn't most males.

'It wasn't, but it's over.' She stopped at her car and unlocked the door.

'Until next time,' he pointed out. 'Rosie, I am concerned about this. It was stated on your job description that flying in a small aircraft would be necessary. Why did you even apply for this job?'

'My reasons for applying for this job have nothing to do with you. I didn't think it would be as much of a problem as it has been, but I promise I'll work on it and the next time there's a call-out, I'm sure I'll be fine.'

'And if you're not? I can't have my staff crumbling to pieces in an emergency situation.'

'It won't happen again,' she said with slow deliberation.

'It had better not.' His voice was firm and brooked no argument. He was a professional and he did his job accordingly. 'I'm responsible for the retrieval team and it's a job I take seriously.'

'And rightly so.'

'Then take this as a warning, Rose. If what happened today happens again, I will have no hesitation in terminating your contract here at Broken Hill Hospital. Understood?'

'Perfectly,' she replied, fighting the lump that was rising in her throat and the angry tears that threatened to spill over her lashes. There was no way in the world she'd let Dave have the satisfaction of seeing her this upset.

With a brisk nod, he turned and strode away. Rose climbed numbly into her car, knowing full well that he'd meant every word he'd said. Not because of the tone of his voice, or his body language, but because he'd called her Rose.

CHAPTER SIX

DAVE dropped into a chair at the kitchen table and slumped forward. He felt like a first-class heel for bawling Rosie out like that, but she'd got him so mad with her ice-maiden attitude he'd felt like throttling her.

He sat up and shook his head in disbelief. One minute she'd been smiling at him and the next snarling. Perhaps it had just been delayed shock? She'd been through enough and he didn't blame her if she felt a little overwrought. Maybe that's all it had been and she'd simply been venting her frustrations at her own inadequacy on him.

He allowed himself to believe it whilst he stood and grabbed a long cool beer from the fridge, accidentally kicking against a chair on his way back to the table. He only drank light beer as he never knew when he'd be needed at the hospital or at an emergency, but right now the coolness of the liquid was what he wanted most.

'Can't you keep it down?' Mick mumbled from the doorway. 'It's after three in the morning.'

'Sorry, bro'.'

'Tough night?'

'Yeah. I suppose you've heard,' Dave said. The locals had an amazing grapevine. In fact, it was worse than any hospital he'd worked in previously. The thought made him smile. Their concern was always genuine and they could always be relied upon to help out in any emergency. Here in the outback, it was often man against the elements.

'Yep. Libby and John's kids. How are they doing?'

'They'll get through.'

'Both off to Adelaide?'

'Yes. Thankfully Penny had just finished her operating

91

list when the call came in so she was able to come out on retrieval with us.'

'She's back in Adelaide now?'

'Yes.'

'Sam will be pleased. Oh, hey, did you manage to get that piece of artwork Penny was after?'

'Yes. She was ecstatic when I told her, and Sam will love it when she gives it to him.'

'Yeah. Hope my wife is as devoted as Penny is to Sam. How did you get the artist to part with it? I thought it wasn't supposed to be for sale?'

'Let's just say he owed me a favour or two,' Dave replied, tapping the side of his nose.

'Most of the people in this district owe you a favour or two.'

'Happens when you save their lives.'

'And now you've got Libby and John to add to the list.'

'It would seem that way.' Dave grinned at his brother before finishing his beer. 'Think I'm about done in.'

'I guess this means you won't be getting up in two more hours to give me a hand with the cattle?'

'You've got it, little brother.' Dave smiled at him and headed towards his room.

'Hey—I almost forgot,' Mick added as he trailed after him. 'Mags called.'

Dave stopped in his tracks at the mention of his ex-wife and turned to face his brother, all traces of humour gone from his face. 'What does she want?'

Mick hesitated.

'Spit it out.'

'All right, but don't shoot the messenger.'

Dave nodded.

'She said she's getting married on Saturday and wants you to know she'll be putting Mel into an exclusive boarding school so the fees will be more expensive than before.'

'What? While she's on her honeymoon? It's school holidays! How long is she going away for?'

Mick shrugged. 'Not sure, but from what she said, it sounds as though it's going to be quite a few months. Her new husband, Julian Moncrief, will be working overseas for a while.'

'Mags is marrying *Julian*?' Dave was astounded and then wondered why he should be surprised.

'They deserve each other. Two peas in a pod.'

'How can you say that, Mick? You only met him once.'

'Twice,' Mick corrected. 'And he was a creep both times.'

'The first would have been at our wedding. When was the second?'

'When I came to Sydney one time. It wasn't long before you and Mags separated.'

'Why don't I remember?'

'You were working all sorts of hours, trying desperately to block out Mags's continual manipulations. I remember you came home one night—aw, it was probably around three or four in the morning and you were dead-dog tired. We sat on the floor on your very expensive rug and just talked. Mags came out just after five and told us both to shut up or get out.'

Dave nodded. '*That* I remember. Soon, I was back here on the farm.'

'Where you belong, mate.'

'Exactly. So when did you see Julian again?'

'He picked Mags up for work. She said her car was on the blink and as his office was across the road from hers, he was…you know…"helping her out".'

Dave didn't miss the underlying meaning. 'Typical.'

'Surprised?'

'I knew about 'em, mate. I confronted her, she didn't deny it, we separated. I'm also sure Julian wasn't the only one.'

'Hurt?'

'Way past it, bro'.' Dave thought for a moment. 'Julian was married then.'

'To his first wife?'

Dave nodded. 'Perhaps you're right, Mick. Perhaps they do deserve each other.'

'And good riddance to them.'

'Yeah, but what about Melody? She's my daughter, too. If Mags thinks she's going to dump Mel into a boarding school, she's got another think coming!'

'What else should she do?'

'Mel can come here.'

'To the farm?' Mick asked. 'It's no place for a kid, Dave. You know that. The last few times Mel has been here, she's been miserable.'

'No, she hasn't.'

'Yes, she has, Dave. If you want Mel to come here for a few months, you'll need to move closer to town.'

'We're only twenty minutes from the town centre and this is my home, too.'

'Mel needs to be with other kids her own age, and if she's coming here to live for a while, it'll take you for ever to get her to school in the morning before you're due at the hospital.'

Dave nodded and rubbed his fingers along his temple 'What exactly did Mags say?'

'She said she'd be putting Mel into the school in the next few days as she had too much to concentrate on with the wedding.'

'This is *so* like her.' Dave slapped his hand against his thigh. 'She fought for custody of Melody when I would have had her at the drop of a hat but, no, Margaret had to have everything *her* way and couldn't possibly have people thinking she wasn't a good mother. This isn't being a good mother and I object to not having a say in what happens to my own daughter. I won't pay those fees.'

'Why not?'

'Because Melody's coming to Broken Hill and that's final.'

'You think that's wise? You know, to rip her out of her environment?'

'She's six years old, Mick. Kids adapt. You and I adapted when our dad walked out on us.'

'Yeah, but we had Mum. We still had a constant in our lives.'

'Don't you remember what mum was like when he left? She fell to pieces,' Dave growled. 'She crumbled into a woman half her previous size and never fully recovered. That's not the point. I won't let Margaret dictate like this. Melody is *my* daughter, too, and I'll go to court if I have to. I'll do whatever it takes, but I will not have my daughter thrust aside in some snotty boarding school, growing up with the belief that neither of her parents wanted her. *I* want her and, believe me, mate, I'm going to get her.'

'What are you going to do?'

'I'll call Mags first thing in the morning and arrange to fly up there in the next few days to pick Melody up.'

'That's the Dunbar fighting spirit,' Mick added, then stopped and looked thoughtfully at his brother. 'You don't think this is what Mags originally wanted? That she'd want you to get on your high horse and demand to take Mel?'

Dave felt his anger rise at Mick's question. He was right. Mags was more than likely manipulating him again. Well, if she wanted to play the game, then it was going to be played by his rules. 'If she persists in going through with this, I'm going to file for full custody and I'll fight her with everything I've got.' He clenched his jaw in determination. 'Mel is my daughter and I love her, Mick. She may not like coming to the farm but I know for a fact that she also loves me.'

'And me! I'm her favourite uncle.'

'You're her only uncle, Mick.'

His brother grinned at him. 'You'll need to get a nanny as well. Or a housekeeper or something. You work such odd hours, mate, you've got to think about Mel's needs.'

Anger surged through Dave at the way his ex-wife still

managed to get to him. 'I can't believe Mags would be so...so... Ugh!' He thumped his fist into the wall and was surprised when it went straight through the old plasterboard.

'That was smart,' Mick remarked ironically, as Dave cradled his hand. 'Get it under some water.'

'It's fine.'

'Don't be a drongo, Dave.'

'I am not an unintelligent, stupid fool.'

'Yeah? Then stop acting like one!'

Dave stormed past his brother, knowing he was right. He shoved his hand under the tap and rinsed it carefully, pleased to see he'd only grazed the skin in a few places. Other than that, all phalanges and the metacarpus seemed to be unbroken.

'How's it look?'

'It'll be fine.'

'You're lucky.'

'Yeah.' He pushed passed Mick and headed to his room. 'Thanks for passing on the message. I'll think about what you've said.'

'Once you get custody of Mel, you shouldn't need to see Mags again.'

'Hadn't thought of that. Maybe she'd want access visits?'

'You think so?'

'Anything's possible with Mags. I've learned never to underestimate that woman. She's capable of anything. It might suit her in years to come to fight for custody of Melody again.'

'Mel's a smart girl, Dave. Hopefully, by then she'll be able to make up her own mind. After all, she's a Dunbar!'

'That she is. Thanks, bro'.' Dave shut his door and lay down on his bed, staring up at the ceiling. What had happened to his well-ordered life? In the last few weeks, it was as though his world had started to spin on an uneven axis.

First Rosie had come along, invading his dreams. Her sweet, pliant lips so delicious to kiss, but that had been before she'd turned into the ice queen. He still had no idea what had happened there.

Now there was Melody. His gorgeous little girl with her long blonde hair and Dunbar blue eyes. He'd seen her just a few weeks ago—at Christmas time. They'd spent the weekend together in Sydney and it had been wonderful.

Mags had seemed glad to have Mel out of the way and now he knew why. Even so, she'd never said anything about getting married again, although it was just like Mags to do things at the last minute like this.

He groaned in exasperation and turned onto his stomach, burying his head beneath the pillow, hoping to stop his mind from being so busy so he could finally get to sleep.

Women—he seemed surrounded by them and they were all a complete mystery to him.

'Morning, darl',' Sadie called as Dave headed onto the ward early Tuesday morning. He'd hardly slept a wink and had got up to help Mick, thankful for the distraction to his thoughts.

'Good morning, Sadie,' he replied, and smothered a yawn.

'What's up, darl'? You look as though you didn't sleep a wink last night.'

'I didn't.'

'What's up? You can tell me, darl'. I was one of your mum's closest friends. Go on, chew my ear.'

'Melody's coming.'

Sadie's eyebrows shot up to her greying hairline. 'Is she now? I didn't think she came in the January holidays.'

'She's coming for good.' He watched as Sadie's jaw hung open.

'You sure that's a good idea, darl'?'

'The best one I've ever had. I should have done it a long time ago.'

'What does Mags think about it?'

'I'll be calling her after ward round to tell her.' Dave slung a stethoscope around his neck as he spoke. 'Let's get the ward round done and get on with the day.'

'Right you are, darl',' Sadie said and patted him affectionately on the back.

True to his word, Dave went to his office after ward rounds and called Mags, surprised to find her awake so early. It would have been close to nine o'clock in Sydney. He didn't beat about the bush and told her up front what he wanted. When she calmly agreed, he knew for a fact that this had all been part of her plan.

'Why didn't you just come right out and say you didn't want her any more? Why can't you at least be honest about Mel?'

'Because then everyone would have thought I was a bad mother. This way, it looks as though—'

'I don't give a stuff how it looks, Mags.'

'Don't call me that. You know I hate it.'

Dave grinned, glad he'd irritated her. 'So you'll agree not to fight me for full custody of Melody?'

'I agree. In fact, my solicitor has already drawn up papers in anticipation of this. They'll be delivered to you by tonight.'

'Geez, Mags. You're…unbelievable.' Dave was completely disgusted with the woman, wondering how on earth he'd ever found her attractive in the first place. 'I'll be there on Thursday to collect her.'

'Don't bother. I've arranged for her to fly out to you.'

'By *herself*! She's six, Mags.'

'Oh, all right, then. I'll send the current nanny with her, too. Happy now? But you're paying for the flights.'

'I'm more than happy to.' Anything. He'd do anything she said at the moment if it meant he could get custody of Mel.

'Right, then. I've got to speak to the caterers.'

The line went dead and Dave looked at the receiver and

shook his head in disbelief. The woman was a piece of work! He called his brother to let him know the progress before heading off to clinic.

Once he'd got through clinic, he grabbed a quick bite of lunch, returning to his office to get his files ready for house calls. The encompassing scent of a very familiar perfume teased at his senses and he looked up to find Rose in his open doorway, her hand raised to knock.

'Good afternoon, Rosie.' He stopped his paper-shuffling, letting his gaze slowly travel over the alluring curves of her body, refreshing his memory. She was dressed in another trouser suit, this time pale blue, and she looked stunning. He could have stayed there for hours, simply watching her, but his self-control, thankfully, got the better of him. He cleared his throat and stood. 'What can I do for you?'

A *lot*! Rose worked hard at not being affected by the touch of his visual caress but she knew she was fighting a losing battle. How did the man have the power to make her knees quiver and her heart turn over with just one look? Then again, how many other women did he look at like that? The thought was enough to help pull her emotions back on track.

'I've just been told by the secretary that my house call list is the same as yours so it makes sense to go together.' When he simply stood there, staring at her as though she'd suggested they rob a bank, Rose pointed to his desk. 'Do you have all the patient files?'

'Yes.' Dave couldn't believe his luck. He got to spend the afternoon with Rosie. Beauty!

'Fine. I'll meet you at your ute.'

'We can take your car if you like.'

'What? Not intimidated by women drivers?'

'Not at all.'

'But I don't know my way around like you do.'

'I can direct you.' He shoved the files into his briefcase, picked up his medical bag, which he'd previously checked, and headed towards her. She quickly stepped out of the doorway, making room for him to pass. 'Let's get going, then.'

They walked out of the hospital together, Rose keeping her distance. She unlocked the car and opened the doors to let the heat out. Dave did the same for the passenger side. A minute later, she closed them again, swatting some flies away from her face. 'Won't take long for it to cool down,' she remarked, as she settled behind the wheel and pulled on her seat belt. Dave did the same and after she'd started the engine, she switched the air-conditioner to 'full'.

'Who's first on the list and which way do I go?' she asked, as she pulled out of the car park.

'Left. Mrs McGill.'

'Mrs McGill.' Rose nodded. 'How did she recover from her food-poisoning experience?'

'All right but it's really aggravated her intestines. I've been watching her closely since just before Christmas when she presented with abdominal pain. When she was brought in with food poisoning, I thought it might have been gallstones, but after doing an ultra sound, I discovered it wasn't.'

'Yet her abdominal pains haven't subsided?'

'Not from what her GP says. I suppose you're seeing her because of the bone cancer,' he stated.

'Yes. Unfortunately, most of the patients I visit at home have a terminal illness.'

'Take the next right turn,' he directed.

She was glad the conversation was kept to medical aspects because that way she could relax a little and enjoy being with him, rather than being forced to remember she was cross with him.

When they arrived at Mrs McGill's, it was to find her lying in bed, moaning in pain. Her husband was quite beside himself. Dave performed her obs while Rose gave her something for the pain.

'That should help,' she said softly. Soon Mrs McGill was more peaceful and started to doze. They headed out to the kitchen, Mr McGill telling them what had transpired that morning and how he'd been about to call the doctor.

'I'd like to admit her to the hospital so I can keep a closer eye on her and run some tests,' Dave said to him. 'Agreed, Rosie?'

'Yes. She can be monitored at the hospital and until the source of this pain is discovered, it'll be best for her.'

'Her oncologist is due here on Thursday so I'll make an appointment for him to stop by her bed and give her a check-up,' Dave told Mr McGill.

They organised Mrs McGill's transfer to hospital then sat down with a cool drink until the ambulance arrived. Once their patient had been handed over to the ambos, they headed to the next appointment.

Three patients later and Rose was ready to call it a day. 'It's hot, I'm tired and these flies are driving me insane,' she told Dave as they waved goodbye at their last house call. 'Which way?' she said at an intersection. 'Once I get back on the main roads, I'm OK.'

'Go right.'

'Thanks.' Rose had been impressed by his relaxed nature towards his patients and it softened her resolve a little. She couldn't let that happen. Forcing herself to concentrate on her driving, Rose worked hard to keep up her cool façade. Now that the patients were out of the way, it was the only shield she had. She was still annoyed with him. She had to remember that. A man shouldn't kiss a woman if he's already involved with another woman. It just isn't the done thing.

First Julian had thought he could do it and now Dave. She could pick them all right. As far as her taste went in men, it was lousy. She was also cross with him for ruining her sleep last night. Just when she'd thought she'd had enough sleepless nights because of him, along had come another one, leaving her feeling washed-out and cranky.

'Left here.' His deep voice broke into her thoughts and washed over her like smooth silk. Rose felt her heartbeat accelerate. Oh, why did he have to have such an effect on her? It wasn't fair. It should be illegal for a man to have such an effect on women—especially a man who was a two-timing snake!

She fixed the image of him kissing Penny firmly in her mind and clung to it, but she could feel herself losing her grip once more. The truth was, the more she saw of Dave, the more she was coming to like him. He was direct and forthright when dealing with staff and patients. He had great skill as a surgeon and as a colleague she admired him greatly. So why did he have to be such a...such a...*male*?

'Rosie,' he said when they were almost at the hospital. She'd been so wrapped in her thoughts that she jumped a little as he spoke. 'Sorry. Didn't mean to startle you.'

Rose slowed down and turned into the hospital car park, pulling into the space she'd vacated a few hours ago.

'We need to talk.' He undid his seat belt and shifted slightly to look at her.

'What about?'

'Us.'

'Dave, there *is* no us.' Rose kept the engine going, hoping he'd take the hint and get out. He didn't.

'Yes, there is, and you know it.'

She looked at him. 'Don't tell me what I know or don't know.'

'There you go again, taking what I say out of context and getting all hot-headed about it.'

'I'm not going to sit here with the engine running and have some hypothetical conversation with you because that's all a relationship between you and I would be—hypothetical. It's hot and I'm tired. Please, get out.'

'Rosie—'

'Now!'

'No. We need to talk and if I have to sit here until the morning, you're going to talk to me.'

'But people will see us toge—'

'I don't care. We need to talk. That's all there is to it.'

He wasn't going to budge on this, she could tell. 'Fine, but…come around to my house where we can at least have some privacy.'

It was obviously an answer he could accept as without another word he got out of her car. 'See you soon, then.' He shut the door and patted the top of her roof. Rose headed off, not at all sure she'd done the right thing.

CHAPTER SEVEN

'TEA or coffee?'

'Tea, please,' he replied, as he settled onto one of the stools at her father's kitchen bench.

Rose moved around the kitchen, feeling Dave's gaze on her the entire time. 'Well?' she asked. 'Are you going to get to the point? After all, you did want to talk.'

'Not when you're in this mood.'

'David!' Her exasperation was now at overload and bubbled over when he laughed.

'All right. It's just hard to talk whilst you're flitting around the kitchen. Why don't we get our cups of tea and go sit in the lounge room?'

'What a good idea.'

'See?'

'See what?'

'I have been known to have them once in a while.'

'What?'

'Good ideas.'

Rose sighed as she handed him his tea and carried her own through to the lounge room. Her next mistake was to sit down on the sofa, thereby leaving room for Dave to come and sit beside her. She tensed for a moment but breathed a sigh of relief when he sat in the armchair opposite her.

'I'm listening,' she said, growing increasingly impatient as well as apprehensive. What was he going to say?

'Firstly, I wanted to apologise for my behaviour last night. I know yesterday evening was difficult for you to get through and you didn't really need the added stress of me bawling you out like that. I still stand by what I said—

104

as head of the retrieval team I must—but I could have waited to speak to you.'

'Thank you.'

'So I'm forgiven?'

Rose nodded. 'For that, but as you said, you had every right to say what you did.'

'Good.' He settled back in his chair.

'Why did you?'

'Why did I what?'

'Why did you bawl me out then and not leave it until today?'

He shifted uncomfortably in his chair and glanced away for a moment. 'I was…well…' he fumbled, and Rose was surprised. 'I was angry with you,' he finally said.

'For causing you so much trouble? I gathered at the time that you weren't that annoyed. You even said you were proud of what I'd done.'

'I was—still am,' he corrected. He leaned forward and placed his cup on the table before standing. 'It's just that…' he started to pace '…before you started to climb up the ladder out of the hole, you seemed…well… receptive to me. Then the next minute—wham!' He slammed one clenched fist into the palm of his other hand for effect. 'I'm being given the cold shoulder. I tried to talk to you, to get you to tell me what was wrong, but, no, you just froze me out. What's worse is you've been doing it ever since.'

Rose clenched her teeth at his words. Why was he talking about this? Surely he knew she must have seen Penny kissing him. He'd looked over at her directly afterwards and had seen her staring.

'So your male ego has taken a hit, eh?' Rose sipped her tea, trying to keep her cool. 'Well, what a shame that is.'

'There you go again. What have I done, Rosie? Tell me.' He walked over and sat down beside her, relieving her of her cup. He placed it on the table and took her hands in his. 'Come on, Rosie. Let's stop playing games. We both know there's this undeniable attraction between us. I know you feel it. The kisses we've shared have told me as much. I may be a little out of practice as far as women go, but I'm not completely immune to the signals.'

Rose wrenched her hands free of his. 'Out of practice? Really? That's not what it looked like to me.'

He frowned. 'What are you talking about?'

Rose stood and walked away from him. She stared unseeingly out the window. 'You and Penny.'

'What?'

'I saw you, Dave. I saw you kiss her when you both came out the hole.'

'You saw *what*? I didn't kiss Penny.'

'Yes, you did. Ask anyone who was there last night. We all saw it.'

Dave frowned as he rose to his feet, then his face relaxed and he laughed. 'Of course.'

'I really don't think this is funny.'

'Penny kissed me when we got out of the hole. Of course!' He hit his forehead as though he should have realised all of this earlier.

'That's right, and you kissed her back.'

'No. I hugged her back. Rosie,' he said laughingly, 'You've definitely got the wrong end of the stick. I'm not involved with Penny.'

'You're not? But…Penny's obviously interested in you.'

'No. Believe me, she's not. Penny is a very happily married woman.'

'She's married?'

'Yes, has been for about ten years now. Her husband, Sam Chadwick, is Head of Orthopaedics at the Adelaide hospital. He's a good friend of mine.'

'Then why was—?'

'Why was Penny kissing me?'

Rose nodded.

Dave shrugged nonchalantly. 'She was thanking me for managing to get a certain piece of artwork Sam had fallen in love with on his last trip here. The artist didn't want to part with it but I managed to persuade him. Penny wants to give it to Sam for his birthday as a surprise.'

'Oh.' Rose felt completely foolish. She knew Dave was a smart man and that he'd realise the jealousy she'd been exhibiting meant she had strong feelings for him—stronger than she'd wanted him to know about.

Dave crossed to her side and lifted her hands, drawing her closer. 'Come here, you gorgeous woman. I've been dying to kiss you for weeks. I can't wait any more, Rosie.'

His mouth was on hers within the next instant. It wasn't a soft or exploratory kiss, as they'd previously shared, but was full of hunger and passion—from both sides. It was as though the last few weeks, working together, the mis-understanding, had all taken its toll and now they were free to hold each other in their arms and take pleasure in the kiss both of them craved.

Rose brought her hands up to his head, her fingers tangling in his hair as his mouth opened over hers once more. Her heart was starting to race out of control and the blood that was pumping at a furious rate around her body was now drumming in her ears.

'Rosie,' he whispered against her lips as he broke free, gasping for breath. 'The real you is much better than any dream.' As he pressed hot kisses on her neck, he savoured the taste of her. It was a delight he could quite easily become addicted to and he quickly pushed the knowledge to the back of his mind.

'Mmm,' Rose groaned with delight, her senses being swept away by the fresh, spicy scent that wound its way around her. As he nibbled at her earlobe, a wave of goose bumps shot down her body and she savoured the sensation.

The next time his mouth met hers, his tongue traced the inner part of her lip causing all the breath to whoosh out of her. The light-headedness made her feel faint and she clung to him as she felt her knees start to give way.

Dave held onto her firmly and she was grateful for his

support. Although, Rose reflected, the hard contours of his chest which were now pressed firmly against her breasts didn't do much to settle her racing heartbeat. She felt the warmth between them, the barrier of their clothes almost non-existent.

'Rosie,' he whispered against her mouth. She liked the way her name sounded on his lips. It was as though he really cared about her and it made her feel…treasured. Whether or not it was another illusion remained to be seen, but for this brief moment Rose decided she was going to enjoy it.

She smiled up at him.

'Hmm? What's funny?'

She shook her head. 'Nothing. I'm just happy.'

'Glad to hear it.' Then, before she could say another word, he swept her off her feet and scooped her into his arms.

'What? Oh!' Rose blushed and took the opportunity to bury her head in his neck. 'You smell so good,' she murmured as he sat them down on the sofa, Rose now settled on his lap.

'So do you, sweetheart.'

'Stop it.' She giggled.

'Really?' He lifted his lips away for a fleeting second.

'No.'

He put them back. Rose closed her eyes, savouring the sensation, trying to recall whether Julian had ever taken the time to nibble at her neck. She couldn't remember. Dave shifted and she leaned back in his embrace, turning her face upwards so their lips could meet.

She sighed, her eyes fluttering closed as the gentle pressure from his mouth relaxed her. She could have stayed here for ever, safe and secure in Dave's arms.

From the sensual haze, a noise broke through. Her mind dismissed it, telling her to concentrate on nothing but Dave and the way he was making her feel.

There it was again! That noise! Her eyes snapped open and she pulled back.

'Rosie?' His voice was sluggish and filled with repressed desire. 'What's wrong?'

'Something's outside.'

Dave listened and when the noise came again he nodded. 'Probably just a bird or a possum.'

'A possum? Here?'

He smiled as he eased her into a more upright position. 'This *is* the outback, sweetheart.' He looked at her startled expression. Her eyes, which had only moments ago been filled with passion, were now as wide as saucers. 'Want to go take a look?'

'Well…uh…I don't know. Is it safe?'

'It's a possum, Rosie, not a drop bear!'

Her eyes grew even wider. 'What's a drop bear? They sound dangerous.'

Dave laughed and helped her to her feet. 'Rosie.' He shook his head sadly. 'You've been living in the city far too long. A drop bear is a tall story that was fabricated to dupe American servicemen during the Second World War.'

'What, killer koalas?' Rose's lips twitched as she saw the humour.

'Something like that. They drop out of the trees onto the shoulders of unsuspecting tourists and hug them to death.' Dave took her hand in his and led the way to the door. 'So as you're not an unsuspecting tourist, I think we'll be safe from the drop bears.' Once outside, Dave let go of her hand and Rose felt momentarily bereft. He walked into the garden and looked up at the roof.

'Just as well it's still daylight saving or we'd be out here with torches,' Dave muttered as she joined him.

'Speak for yourself. I'd be hibernating inside, hoping it came nowhere near me.'

'Aha. Over there.' Dave pointed to the drainpipe as the

possum scuttled down it and onto the verandah. It looked at them as if to say, Go on, I dare you.

'Cute, isn't it?' Dave whispered.

'You think so?' Rose wasn't quite sure. Little furry creatures weren't really her cup of tea.

'We need to watch where it goes. If it gets into your roof, it can cause all kinds of havoc.'

'What do we do? Call the fire brigade? The ranger or…or someone?' Rose gripped tightly to Dave's arm.

'Rosie? It's just a possum. Sure, it can damage property and be a pest but it's a *possum*. That's all.'

'I'll bet its claws are sharp.'

'They are.' He turned and headed over to his ute, keeping the noise down as he went.

'Wh-what are you doing?' Rose followed him, keeping a close eye on the possum.

'We'll distract it with some food and then I'll grab it.'

'*We?* Who's this *we*? I'm not going near that thing.'

Dave frowned at her. 'It's a *possum*, Rosie.'

'So? I don't mind looking at pictures of them in a book but me and furry little things just don't go together.' There was a hint of indignation in Rose's tone but she kept her gaze trained on the possum, glancing at Dave every few seconds. 'What are you going to do with it once you've caught it?'

'Let it go in the bush. I'll put it in a cardboard box and set it free on my way home.'

'I take it you've done this before.'

'Sure,' he replied matter-of-factly. He pulled out a pair of heavy-duty gloves. 'Your dad should have a box I can use in his shed. You stay here and watch it and I'll go and get the box and some food.'

'No.' Rose was by his side in an instant.

'Rosie, we need to keep an eye on it in case it moves. We need to know where it goes or it'll end up in your roof and that's when the costs start mounting up. Possum removal is high in this neck of the woods. Look, you go inside and make some possum food and *I'll* stay and watch it.'

'Possum food? I don't know what possums eat?'

'Exactly, yet you have two eyes and can watch a possum. Can't you?' Dave took a deep breath and turned to face her. 'You'll be fine.' He kissed the tip of her nose. 'Trust me.'

Rose eyed him with suspicion. The smirk on his face told her he was enjoying this and she wasn't one hundred per cent sure he wasn't pulling her leg. 'Well…what do I do if it moves?'

'Just watch it, Rosie. Watch where it goes.'

'And if it goes into the roof?'

'Then it goes into the roof and we take it from there.' Dave peeled her hand from his arm. 'You'll be fine. I'll be back before you know it.'

Rose kept her gaze on the possum, watching in her peripheral vision as Dave walked slowly to the front door and opened it. The possum moved—only slightly—towards him and for a split second Rose thought it was going to follow him into the house. 'Drop bear,' she muttered. 'More like feral furry things.'

She was growing more and more impatient with every passing second that Dave was gone. 'Come on. Hurry up,' she whispered to herself. The possum was keeping a close eye on her as well and Rose could almost see its little mouth curving into a grin. The cheeky thing was laughing at her.

'You OK?'

'Ah-h!' Rose screamed at the sound of another woman's voice. The possum moved, shooting up the drainpipe as fast as it could. Dave came bursting through the front door and raced onto the grass.

'Rosie?' he called, and then stopped dead in his tracks. 'Evening, Mrs Fredrick.' He nodded politely. He could see Rosie was trembling and walked over to pat her shoulder.

'It's all right,' he murmured, his eyes lighting with laughter.

'You OK?' Mrs Fredrick repeated. 'She all right, Dave?' she asked when she received no reply from Rose.

'Just trying to get a possum out. I think you scared poor Rosie.'

'Oh, sorry, Rosie. Didn't mean to be sneaking up on you like that.'

'She'll be fine, Mrs Fredrick.' He patted Rose's shoulder again. 'Where did the possum go?' he asked.

Rose shivered again and pointed to the drainpipe.

Dave walked to that part of the house, his expression concerned. It quickly cleared. 'No. It's all right. He's not in the roof, I can see him.' He dashed for the door. 'Let me get the food. We'll try and coax him down. Stay with Rosie, please, Mrs Fredrick.' With that, he was gone again.

'Nasty pests, these possums,' Mrs Fredrick said. 'Cute to look at and nice in their own environment but I'll tell you, they can rip the inside of your roof to shreds in no time at all. Usually it's just because they're scared, poor things, and want to get out as much as you want them out.'

Rose shuddered. 'Please, stop talking about them.'

'You don't like them?' Mrs Fredrick's eyebrows shot upwards in surprise.

'Not particularly.' Rose could feel herself calming down a fraction but she wouldn't be completely calm until that possum was long gone from the house. It appeared that Dave was going to be her knight in shining armour yet again and she wasn't going to dispute the fact one little bit. To own the truth, she rather liked it. He'd saved her from food poisoning and now a possum. A smile touched her lips as he came out of the house, holding a plate with something on it.

'What's he got?' she asked Mrs Fredrick.

'Probably some sort of fruit, soaked with wine or some other form of alcohol. Berries are the best—raspberries in vodka is one of the best ones.'

'What? Doesn't that hurt the poor animal?'

'Ah, no. Just gets them a little drunk so we can take them back to the bush without them tearing us to shreds. Concerned about the native animals, eh? There's hope for you yet.'

'I'm a doctor, Mrs Fredrick. I care about life—even if it's not human.'

'Dave would never hurt an animal. Not unless he absolutely had to.'

'What do you mean?'

'Well, out here, if you hit a roo, for example, the kindest thing you can do to the poor animal is put it out of its misery.'

'Eww!' Rose couldn't believe she was hearing this. What on earth had possessed her to come to Broken Hill in the first place? She must have been out of her mind. She knew that spending time with her dad was paramount but he was off on his honeymoon and here she was, trying to make sure a possum didn't get into the roof. Correction—here *Dave* was, making sure a possum didn't get into the roof.

He was a good man and they were *definitely* hard to come by.

She watched as Dave held the plate up towards the possum and then placed it on the ground before heading in their direction.

'What did you give it?'

'Eh?'

'The possum food. What is it?'

'Banana and scotch.'

'Oh.'

'I take it by that reply that Mrs Fredrick has been doing some explaining?' He watched as Mrs Fredrick nodded. 'Thanks. Poor Rosie here isn't used to all these non-city things that happen.'

'Most city slickers aren't.' Mrs Fredrick shook her head sadly as she spoke.

'Ah, but Dr Partridge here has told me she's not really a city slicker. She's apparently lived in the sticks.'

'Really? Where?' Mrs Fredrick asked.

'Wagga Wagga,' Rose supplied a little absent-mindedly, as the possum started to move down the drainpipe towards the food.

Dave and her neighbour laughed. 'That's not the outback, Rosie. *This*…' He spread his arms out wide. '*This* is the outback.'

'Look, he's eating it!' She said with surprise.

'Of course he is. I make the best possum food.'

'Perhaps you should think of opening a restaurant for them, then.'

'Cute. Very cute, Rosie. All right, so now we watch him and wait.'

'How long will it be before the alcohol takes effect?'

'About ten minutes or so,' he answered, and Mrs Fredrick nodded her agreement.

'So we just stand here and wait?'

'You've got it.'

'Is the box all ready?' Mrs Fredrick asked.

'It's around the back with the gloves. I'll go through the house, around and out the back and then come along the side of the house, over here.' He pointed to where the possum was now happily munching away on the banana.

'Good boy,' Mrs Fredrick replied. 'You all right now, Rosie?' she queried again.

Rose forced a smile. 'I will be, Mrs Fredrick, as soon as that possum has gone.'

'Just as well Dave was here to help out.'

Rose could tell by her neighbour's tone that she was mightily interested in what was really going on between the two of them, and Rose wasn't quite sure what she wanted people to know.

'Just as well,' she agreed mildly. 'Has it finished yet?'

'Yep. Cleaned up the plate.' Dave preened. 'Told you I make good possum food.'

Rose laughed softly. 'I'm sure it looks good on your résumé.'

'What—the possum food itself, or the fact that I can make it?' Dave chuckled.

'Well, as you've got the situation well in hand, I'll go back inside out of the heat. Have a nice evening—the pair of you,' Mrs Fredrick said with a knowing grin, before heading off towards her own home.

'Gossip out here is more potent than any hospital I've ever worked in,' Dave said quietly, as they both watched the possum.

'So I've gathered,' Rose replied.

They waited. Side by side, swatting flies, their arms brushing occasionally. Rose could feel the heat radiating from Dave and now that they were alone again she gave her senses permission to enjoy it. She shifted slightly and their hands brushed against each other. Dave didn't move away but stayed where he was.

'I'd like nothing better than to take you in my arms and kiss you goodnight, Rosie, but I think we need to protect your reputation for a little longer—at least until your father gets home.'

'How chivalrous of you.'

'Yes, I thought so.'

'Modest, too.'

'Absolutely.' Dave chuckled. 'Look.' He pointed to where the possum was starting to slump a bit. 'I think it's almost time.' He felt for her fingers and gave them a quick squeeze. 'I'm glad I came.'

'So am I.'

'Really?'

'Yes.' Rose glanced up at him. 'And not just because of the possum.'

He smiled down at her. 'Are you free for dinner tomorrow night?'

'Yes,' she replied a little hesitantly.

'What's wrong?'

'I just don't know if I want to go out in public yet. Do you know what I mean?'

'Yes. You could come out to the farm and I could rustle you up a plate of steak and egg.'

'Mmm,' she replied, pulling a sour face. 'Sounds… appetising.'

Dave laughed but as he mentioned the farm, he remembered that Melody would be arriving in two days' time. Tomorrow night would be the last time he could go out without having to worry about making babysitting arrangements. 'Yes, we definitely need to see each other tomorrow night. We have a lot to…discuss.'

Rose was glad he wanted to see her again but was slightly puzzled by the underlying vehemence in his words. Still, he was right. They *did* have a lot to discuss and she wanted to make sure he understood that whatever this was brewing between them had to be taken at a snail's pace. She wasn't going to let her heart be swept away this time. She was going to guard it and move slowly—as she should have done previously.

'Why don't you come here for dinner?'

'The neighbours will see my ute and know I'm here.'

'They already know that much,' Rose countered. 'But at least this way we won't be under a microscope.'

'Good point. All right. I'll call by after clinic. What time are you due to finish tomorrow?'

'The urology list usually finishes on time so I should be home just after five-thirty.'

'All right. Can I bring anything?'

'Yes. Any other tools you might need in case the house is ridden with other furry creatures.'

He laughed. 'You're a good sport, Rosie Partridge. That's what I like about you.' He squeezed her hand once more before finally letting go. 'Let me get this one out of here for you.'

The possum was now about to fall asleep but even so, Rose kept her distance. Dave went through the house and soon materialised around the side where the possum was, his heavy-duty gloves on his hands, the box standing by.

With little effort or struggle, he picked the dozing possum up and placed it carefully into the box. Folding the lid over, he made sure there was enough air circulating for the animal before carrying it towards his car.

Rose scooted out of the way and watched as he put the box on the front passenger seat. 'Is that a good idea?' she called.

He turned and gave her a slow but encompassing smile. She felt her insides warm at the sight. 'Worried about me? Don't be. This little fella will be asleep for the next hour at least. If I put him in the back and the box lid flies open, he might be attacked by a predator. I'll take care of him, Rosie.'

'Oh. OK. See you tomorrow.'

'Sleep sweet, Rosie.'

'You, too,' she responded. Rose turned away and walked to the front door but couldn't resist turning to watch him drive away. He tooted the horn and stuck his arm out the open window to wave. She waved back, a silly schoolgirl grin on her face.

Rose opened the door and, out of curiosity, glanced over to Mrs Fredrick's house. As she did, she saw the lace curtains fall back into place. She shook her head, surprised to find that she didn't really mind all that much. Dave made her happy and that was something she hadn't experienced in a long time.

The instant she stepped inside, the phone rang. She reached for the receiver, hoping it wasn't the hospital with an emergency.

'Hello, princess,' her father's deep voice boomed down the line. 'How are things going?'

'Oh, fine, Dad. Just fine—now.'

'What's been going on, Rosie?' She told him about the possum and how Dave had taken care of the situation. 'Just as well he was there, then,' her father said, and she noted a strangeness in his tone.

'Yes, it was.'

'Has he…you know…stopped by before?'

Rose frowned. 'Only when I had food poisoning, but I've already told you about that. Why do you want to know?'

'I think young Dave has taken a shine to you,' her father said.

Her frown changed to a smile. 'You think so?'

'Rosie.' His tone was even more curious. 'What aren't you telling me?'

'A lot of things, Dad. How's Beverley?'

'Beautiful.' Her father sighed like a man in love should. 'Simply beautiful.'

Wanting to get him off the topic of Dave and herself, Rose asked, 'So what have you been doing today? Lazing around a swimming pool, sipping cocktails?'

Reg chuckled. 'Something like that.' He then launched into a full-scale account of what they'd been doing since he'd last spoken to Rose, and while he was talking, she fixed herself some dinner, stretching the cord of the phone as far as she could. Over half an hour later, she rang off and sat down to eat her food. No sooner had she put the first forkful in her mouth than the phone rang again.

'Dr Partridge.'

'Rosie! Thank goodness.' The sound of Dave's voice warmed her right down to her toes and she forgot all about her dinner. 'I was starting to get concerned when I couldn't get through. Had you accidentally knocked the receiver off the hook?'

'No. My father called.'

'They're enjoying themselves, I hope?'

'Yes.'

'Listen, I wanted to let you know that the possum in question is now safe and back in its natural habitat.'

'And you made sure he was well hidden so he wouldn't be attacked by a dingo or something?'

'Absolutely.'

'Good.'

Dave laughed. 'You really are a mixture, aren't you?'

'A mixture of what?' she asked cautiously.

'You aren't the adventurous type at all yet your natural concern shows that you care.'

'So?' She was defensive now.

'I'm not criticising you, Rosie. I'm saying I like it. My ex-wife didn't like to venture out of her comfort zone and couldn't care less about anyone who did.'

Rose didn't miss the bitterness in his tone. 'I know what you mean,' she replied, thinking of Julian.

'Been there, experienced that?' he queried lightly.

'Yes.' Her voice was soft.

'Did he hurt you?'

'If you mean did he break my heart? I thought he had but now I'm not so sure.' If Dave had asked her that question one month ago, she would have answered in the affirmative. After tonight, with Dave's kind and caring attitude, Rose knew Julian hadn't broken her heart as she was still able to feel. 'I think he dented my ego more,' she acknowledged honestly.

'I know how that feels.' He laughed without humour.

'How about you? Did your ex-wife break your heart?'

'She gutted me from the inside, twisted me into knots and discarded me without a thought.'

'Really? When? Sorry, I didn't mean to pry, it's just that you seem so…so…well, together.'

'We divorced over six years ago, Rosie. Time is a great healer of wounds. I'm not so sure about anger but wounds—definitely.'

'You don't like her?'

'No. I can't say she's one of my favourite people.'

'Regrets?'

'We all have them, sweetheart.'

'Bitterness?'

'No. I've forgiven Mags for hurting me and for the way she disrespected our marriage vows.'

Rose grasped his meaning quickly and as she knew Dave was bound to a life of chivalry, he'd also be bound to monogamy as well.

'That doesn't mean I like her or want to spend time with her,' he added.

'Do you see her often?'

'No, but I speak to her a few times a year.'

'Why?' Rose wasn't too sure whether she should have asked the question but felt if ever she was going to pry into Dave's past, now was the time. He'd been the one to open the conversation of past relationships. Besides, if he didn't want to answer, she was sure he'd say so.

'Divorce is never easy when there's a child involved.' As Dave said the words, he held his breath. There, it was out. Rosie now knew he had a child. There was silence on the other end of the phone and he closed his eyes as he waited for her to speak. After seeing how she'd reacted with young Joe the other week, he wasn't too sure how she'd receive this news. 'Kids and I just don't mix.' That's what she'd said.

'You have a child?' she said finally, unable to believe it. A divorced man with a family. Warning bells sounded. It was on her list—her list of what to avoid at all costs— yet she was finding it increasingly difficult to adhere to *that* list. Why hadn't she heard anything about this at the hospital? Probably, she reminded herself, because she didn't listen to gossip.

'I have one child. Melody is her name and she's six years old.'

CHAPTER EIGHT

'SIX?' Rose felt herself start to tremble a bit. Kids made her uncomfortable. She wasn't good with them. She was just like her mother—hopeless with children. She pushed the thoughts aside roughly. 'But I thought you'd been divorced for—' She cut herself off. 'I'm sorry, Dave. It's really none of my business.'

'I think it is, Rosie. I like you. I want to pursue a relationship with you. I don't know where it will lead but there it is, nevertheless. So let's get the past out into the open so we can move forward.' She was silent again. 'Rosie? I didn't mean to dump all of this on you straight away but isn't it better that we find things out now, rather than later? After you thinking I was involved with Penny, I don't want any other misunderstandings to surface.'

Rose listened to what he said, agreeing with him. 'Is this what you wanted to talk about tomorrow night?'

'Something like that.'

'Melody,' she said softly. 'Nice name.'

'She's a nice girl.'

She could tell Dave was smiling. He obviously thought the world of his daughter and it improved her opinion of him.

'Mags chose the name. She's the type of woman who has to have control over everything and thought a child would fit nicely into her new life. After all, a few of her friends had babies and they made it sound so special and unique. It was like a red flag to a bull and she couldn't resist.

'The conception happened during our last attempt to reconcile our marriage. Little did I know that she'd planned

121

the entire thing.' Dave shook his head as he remembered the way Mags had used him. 'I woke up one morning and she was gone. No note. No phone call. No nothing. I contacted the solicitor, as that was the only number I had to track her down, and he informed me that Margaret saw no further need to remain in the relationship and that divorce proceedings would commence once the proper procedures had been satisfied.'

'But what about the baby?'

'She told me I was the father—after Melody's birth. I didn't even see my daughter until she was eight weeks old. By then Mags had realised that motherhood wasn't all it was cracked up to be. She hired a nanny, fought and won custody and that was that.'

'Can you be sure…? What I mean is… Is she—?'

'Is she mine? Yes. I had tests done to prove it and she's mine all right.'

Rose didn't miss the vehemence in his words. 'How often do you see her?'

'Quite a lot. I miss her like crazy but a broken marriage is just a part of our lives.'

'Must be rough, being so far away from her.'

'It is.'

'I presume they're in Sydney?'

'That's right.'

'So do you go there or does your daughter come here?'

'Both. It all depends. In fact…' Dave paused for a moment and took a deep breath '…she's coming on Thursday.'

'Thursday? *This* Thursday?'

'Yes.'

'But that's in two days' time.' Rose couldn't believe what she was hearing. She pulled the receiver away from her ear and stared at it. Who was this man? It brought back the reality that she really knew nothing about him— except for the uncharacteristic physical attraction that had flared up between them.

'I know. I was going to fly to Sydney and get her but Mags is sending her here with the current nanny.'

Rose had no idea what to say. He was divorced. He had a daughter—a daughter who was coming to town. She opened and closed her mouth like a goldfish—completely stunned by what he was saying.

'Rosie?' he said when she didn't respond. 'I know this is a lot but, as I said, I want it all out in the open.'

'How…how long will she be here for?'

He cleared his throat. 'For ever—hopefully.'

'What?'

'That is if Mags doesn't change her mind.'

'Dave, this is a lot for me to deal with.'

'I know and, fair dinkum, Rosie, I'm sorry,' he said softly, knowing he was only causing her more confusion. 'I know this is a lot for you to handle, especially as we've only just started…whatever this is that's sprung up between us. The best advice I could probably give you is to keep well away from me, but that's not what I want.'

'Why?'

'Because you're the first woman I've been remotely interested in for the last six years.'

Rose didn't know what to say. This time, though, her silence was due to overwhelming surprise. He liked her. He *really* liked her. Rose felt her insides turn to mush. He'd seen her when she'd been tired and rude, sick, gripped with fear and he *still* liked her.

'Rosie?'

'Hmm? Uh…thank you. That's really nice of you to say that but, um…that's not what I meant when I asked why.'

'What did you mean, then?'

'Why will your daughter be staying for good?'

'Because Mags is getting married again. Her wedding is this Saturday and she can't be bothered having Mel around any longer.'

'That's horrible.' Rose wasn't overly confident with

children but she knew this was a terrible thing to do to a child. 'So you offered to take her, naturally.'

'Actually, Mags was planning to put her into boarding school.'

'What? She's six years old.'

Dave smiled. Rosie really was on his wavelength. 'My sentiments exactly.'

'So you're going to apply for full custody?'

'Yes. When I told Mags I wanted custody of Mel, she told me she'd already started proceedings. The papers have been drawn up. They were supposed to have arrived to-night but obviously the courier got lost. Hopefully, I'll get them tomorrow but the waiting is starting to tear me apart. I wasn't planning on doing anything until Melody arrived but it appears Mags had other plans. Still, she has been known to change her mind in the past so until I get those papers it isn't going to be an easy ride.'

'How long are they planning to honeymoon?'

'Julian—her new husband-to-be—is in the computer business and has plans to work overseas. This is all ac-cording to Mags, so who knows how much of it is true?'

Rose almost fell off her chair. Her dinner was com-pletely forgotten as Dave's words almost paralysed her. 'Did…did you say Julian?' Her voice was barely audible. She bit her lower lip, realising belatedly that it was trem-bling.

'That's right.' He heard her gasp and the tone of her voice made him sit up straighter—aware that something wasn't right. 'What's wrong? Rosie?'

'Julian Moncrief?' she whispered.

'You *know* him?'

'I was engaged to him three months ago.'

That certainly explained a lot. Dave replaced the receiver in the cradle after Rosie had quickly said she'd better go. Her tone had been full of distraught emotion and when he'd offered to come back around, she'd been adamant in her refusal. He didn't blame her. No one wanted to have their soul bared to a relative stranger like himself.

No. He and Rosie *weren't* strangers. Sure, there were things they didn't know about each other but he refused to say they were strangers. Tonight had changed that for good.

Dave stalked over to the fridge and grabbed a beer, taking it out onto the verandah. He leaned against the rail. Knowing that Julian had been a part of Rosie's past explained a lot about the woman herself. He wouldn't blame her if she avoided him simply because he was divorced. Julian had been divorced—twice.

Dave raised the beer to his lips. Knowing the type of person Julian was, he could guess how that man had behaved towards Rosie, but he knew how to fix it. He needed to show her that he wasn't like that two-timing swine. He might be divorced—just like Julian was. He might have one child—Julian had three. But, unlike Julian, he was trustworthy and wanted to be a part of his daughter's life. Julian had written off his children years ago.

There was also the problem that Rosie felt uncomfortable around children. He frowned, unsure whether he should be concerned about that. There was obviously a reason why Rosie was like this.

How could Reg have let his daughter grow up without playing with other kids? And what had happened to her mother? All he knew about Reg was that he had been divorced, never spoke about his ex-wife and had one child. Perhaps Rose's parents' divorce had emotionally scarred her in some way.

There were too many unanswered questions and it intrigued him more. A primitive protective urge came over him when he thought about Rosie. He'd helped her through food poisoning—and she'd let him. He'd helped her with her mild claustrophobia—and she'd let him. He'd helped her with the possum—and she'd let him. Yet for all that, she was still a woman who could stand on her own two feet and she'd proved that by the way she'd come through each of those situations. Everyone needed help at some point in their lives and it was refreshing to find that Rosie wasn't adverse to allowing others to help her.

Would she let him help her relax around children?

Rose finally threw back the bedcovers in disgust and headed to the shower as the clock ticked over to six a.m. What was the point of lying in bed any longer when she'd only been pretending to sleep?

She sighed as she stepped into the shower stall and turned her face up to the spray, hoping the soothing warm water would do something to relax her. 'Not good, waking up this agitated,' she mumbled to herself. She'd thought that after those wonderful kisses from Dave she might have managed a better night's sleep. 'And then he phoned.' Rose shook her head.

She had mixed emotions about the news of Julian's wedding. It was just so typical of him. He'd been married and divorced twice when she'd met him. Within two months of them starting to date, he'd proposed and, like a complete idiot, she'd been swept away by his sophistication and charm and had instantly accepted.

Then she'd discovered the truth about him. He'd started criticising the way she'd dressed and the long hours she'd spent at the hospital. He'd also told her that once they were married, he expected her to give up her career and move if he needed to move.

Being in the computer business, he needed to be mobile, he'd told her. It was important to him to have a wife who'd make a good hostess, and with her classic looks and poise, he'd decided she fitted the bill.

'He won't be faithful to you,' his first wife had told her and the second wife had confirmed. When Julian had made excuses about working late and cancelling their dinner reservations, she'd begun to suspect. Her suspicions had been confirmed when she'd followed him one evening and found he'd been meeting another woman—a woman she'd discovered was called Margaret.

When Rose had next spoken to his first wife, she'd confirmed that Margaret was a long-standing favourite of Julian's and that, regardless of who he'd been married to, Margaret had always been in the wings.

Now Rose discovered that this Margaret woman was Dave's ex-wife! He'd implied that she'd cheated on him—obviously with Julian. She shook her head, snapping herself out of the thoughts that had been spinning around all night long, and reached for the shampoo.

'Work. Concentrate on work. Julian is out of your life. You've moved on. Dave is nice. Dave likes you and Dave appears to be honest.' Rose washed her hair vigorously, speaking her thoughts out loud. 'Dave is also divorced and the father of one. You shouldn't get involved with him. He's all wrong for you. Then again, what man is really honest? Do they even exist?' She only knew one man who was honest and he'd been duped himself by a dishonest woman. 'Seems to work both ways, Dad,' she told the shower wall, and sighed heavily.

Dave had a child. This was something Rose hadn't counted on. She'd always wondered whether she was like her mother deep down inside—her mother who'd abandoned her father and herself. Rose had been just over three years old when her mother had left and when she'd questioned her father about it later, he'd said that her mother's excuse had been that she 'wasn't the maternal type'.

Her father had wanted children and her mother had obliged but had hated every minute of it. One day, she'd upped and left and Rose had never seen or heard from her again. A part of her had always been curious and her father, bless him, had answered all her questions lovingly and honestly, showing her photographs of the woman she now looked almost identical to.

Was she identical in behaviour as well? Rose had never had much to do with children in the past and she'd tried never to think about if she'd ever be a mother herself. Having grown up without one, she had no idea how they were supposed to behave. Her mother's behaviour had been appalling—according to her father—and he'd blamed himself for the way Rosie had been treated.

'Agh! Stop it,' she told herself as she switched off the taps.

After her shower, Rose decided she needed a good breakfast. 'Surely that will help improve my mood.'

The phone rang as she was in the middle of sautéing some onions for the frittata she was planning to make. She glanced at the clock as she snatched it up. At six-thirty, it could only be the hospital.

'Dr Partridge.'

'Good morning, my sweet Rosie. I just needed to hear your voice,' Dave said. His rich, deep voice washed over her and she momentarily closed her eyes, savouring the feeling.

'There you go. You've heard it. What are you doing up so early?'

'Early? I'm always up at six, sometimes earlier if Mick needs help with things. Besides,' he added in a softer tone, 'I couldn't sleep. I was worried about you.'

Rose smiled. 'Well, thank you for worrying about me, but I'm fine. Hang on a minute.' She stretched the phone cord over towards the stove. 'Don't want the onions to burn.'

'What are you cooking? Are you as good as your father?'

'I'm making breakfast frittata and, no, I'm not as good as my father…but he taught me everything I know,' she added.

'Right. Breakfast at your house. See you soon.'

Rose laughed, loving the way a few minutes talking to him had put her in a better mood. 'Dave, you can't come around for breakfast. What will the neighbours think?' It was then she heard the 'disconnected' signal. 'Dave?'

He'd hung up on her. What a cheek! 'Oh, no,' she said as she replaced the receiver. 'He's coming around!'

Rose wasn't sure what to do first. She was thankful that she'd showered and was presentably dressed, although, with Dave's easygoing nature, she doubted whether that would be of any importance to him. He *was* so different from Julian. He might be divorced, he might have a child, but he was still very different. At times like these, she had no idea how to behave.

Should she be the cool, calm sophisticate who was used to men popping in for breakfast? Should she be hard and unyielding, refusing to let him in when he arrived? 'Just concentrate on the cooking or all he's going to be turning up for is burnt offerings,' she told herself firmly.

By the time she heard his vehicle, breakfast was ready but she was nowhere near the same. What if one of the neighbours saw him? What if they thought his ute had been parked out front all night long?

What was going to happen when they saw each other again? Was it going to be awkward? No. Not with Dave. He wouldn't let it be awkward. She'd only ever had polite, predictable relationships, she realised with a start. The men she'd dated before Julian had all been professionals. Polished. Seemingly perfect. Perhaps that's what had been missing from her life? A bit of spontaneity. With Dave, she had no idea whether she was coming or going. It was a strange but not unpleasant feeling and right now, although her stomach was alive with butterflies at the thought of seeing him again, she was looking forward to it at the same time.

His coming would bring the gossips out in force but she knew there really wasn't anything she could do about the rumour mill of Broken Hill. Right now, she had a hungry man knocking loudly at her front door.

'I'm coming,' she called a little impatiently when his knocking didn't stop. She wrenched open the door and gasped with surprise as he burst through, swept her into his arms and kicked the door shut in one swift motion. Before she could say anything else, his lips were on hers, devouring them hungrily.

Rose wasn't complaining. The same urge had built within her from the moment he'd left yesterday evening and she moaned with delight as his arms tightened around her back, moulding her body to his.

Her breathing was ragged, matching his. Her body was on fire, liquid heat spreading throughout her body. How did he manage to fuel such an uncharacteristic response in her with a few simple kisses? They weren't simple, she corrected. They were the most passionate kisses she'd ever received in her life—and she *loved* them.

Finally, his mouth broke free from hers. 'You taste and smell delicious.'

Rose smiled shyly up at him. 'That's the food, silly.'

'No.' Dave was serious as he looked down into her up-turned face. 'You are one very beautiful woman, Rosie Partridge, and don't let anyone tell you differently.' He kissed her again before letting her go and taking two big steps away. 'If I don't put some distance between us, breakfast will be the last thing we'll be concentrating on this morning.'

Rose felt herself blushing and looked way. 'Is that so?' She worked hard to inject a haughty note into her tone but wasn't sure she'd succeeded. 'How do you know I'd let you do anything other than kiss me or eat the food I've cooked?' She turned away from him and headed into the kitchen.

'I should hope you wouldn't.' He chuckled as he followed her. 'I just love it when you come across all prim and proper like that.' He grabbed her from behind and held her back against his chest. He bent and nibbled at her earlobe, which sent a wave of goose bumps spreading down one side of her body. 'All I meant,' he whispered seductively, 'is that you're so…addictive, I doubt I'll ever be able to get enough of you.'

'I knew what you meant,' she told him, not entirely sure she wanted to pull away. Even if she did, would her own legs support her? 'Let's eat. I don't want you to be late for ward round. Then people will *really* start asking questions.'

'So nice to be with a woman who understands my job.' Dave reluctantly let her go and sat down on a stool.

'Your ex-wife didn't?' Rose concentrated on making sure everything was ready and pulled the frittata from beneath the grill.

'No. Mags resented my work as a doctor.'

'Then why did she marry you?'

'Good question. Apparently, it was considered fashionable to be a doctor's wife.'

'How did you meet?' She served the food up and put a plate in front of him.

'Looks and smells delicious,' he said, and took one of her hands in his. Slowly, he raised it to his lips and pressed a light kiss on her knuckles. Rose smiled, a little confused but flattered all the same. 'Thanks for letting me in.'

'How could I not?' She laughed. 'If I hadn't, I'm sure you would have knocked the door down.'

Dave laughed, before taking a bite. 'Probably. Mmm, this is great! What's in it?'

She wondered whether he was trying to avoid answering the question and decided she'd let him—for the moment. If he wanted to pursue a relationship with her, then she had the right to ask him personal questions. 'Potato, bacon, eggs, onion and sun-dried tomato—oh, and some herbs.'

'It's delicious. You *are* as good a cook as your father.'

'Thank you for saying so, even if I don't agree. I've had a lifetime of eating his cooking and somehow it always tastes better than anything I ever make. Still, he would always encourage me.'

'And that's the point. To try new things.' Dave swallowed his mouthful and looked at her, his gaze tearing a path directly to her soul.

'Is that what you're doing with me?' she asked softly. 'Trying something new?'

His fork clattered to his plate and he reached for her hand again. 'Rosie, I would never intentionally hurt you but, yes, I guess I am trying to try something new—if that makes sense. As I said, I haven't been involved with a woman since Mags so, in essence, I *am* trying something new. I'm trying to see whether this natural chemistry that exists between us is just physical or something more.'

'And if it *is* just physical?'

'We'll cross that bridge when we come to it.'

She retrieved her hand. 'That's not good enough, Dave.' Rose took a bite of her breakfast. She forced herself to chew calmly and swallow, before elaborating. 'It's only been three months since Julian broke off the engagement. You've had six years to recover from your busted relationship.'

Dave nodded. 'The situation with Julian has made you question your own judgement.'

'Yes.'

'That never goes away, Rosie. I'm *still* questioning my judgement. We should all question our judgement. It's the only way we learn. In our profession, we've learned what we need to do to save people's lives. It's our experience that helps us through in difficult times but we still question things. If we didn't and the patient wasn't a textbook case, they'd probably die. It's part of life, it's part of any relationship. I think the real problem is that for a while there we *stopped* questioning our judgement.'

He started eating again. 'You want to know how I met Mags?'

Rose didn't reply, she just forked in another mouthful and waited. If he wanted to tell her, she would listen, but she wouldn't have initially asked the question if she didn't want to know.

'She was a patient of mine. She had a badly busted appendix which perforated on the table. She was extremely ill for a while but thankfully she recovered. Once she was discharged from my care, she kept stopping by the hospital to see me. The rest, as they say, is history. How about you and Julian?'

Rose took a sip of her orange juice. 'He was supplying the hospital with new computers and devising a special program for the secretaries to use. We kept bumping into each other in the staff cafeteria and one day we sat together and had lunch. The next day, he took me out to lunch and the next thing I knew he was proposing and I'd accepted.'

'Fast.' He nodded again. 'That's the way Julian works.'

'So I gather.'

'Are you hurt that he's found someone else so soon?'

'No. His previous wives told me all about Margaret. Apparently he's been seeing her on and off for years.'

'You know his ex-wives?'

'Yes. They started calling me after our engagement was announced. At first I thought they were being vindictive— at least that's what Julian had said when I told him they'd been calling. Then I realised they were just trying to save me from what they'd been through.'

'He was at my wedding. A friend of Mags's. He was married to his first wife then. She seemed nice but I didn't see her again. Julian's the type of man who needs a pretty woman at his side who'll put up with his many indiscretions. She'll be the apple of his eye so long as she does what he wants.'

'You think Margaret fits the bill?'

He shrugged. 'They're too much alike. Both like to play the field. Both are manipulative. Good luck to them. I truly don't care. So long as I get custody of Mel, I'll be happy.'

At the mention of his daughter, Rose swallowed suddenly and started coughing. Dave patted her on the back. 'OK?'

She had a quick drink and nodded.

'I mention my daughter and you start to choke. Is

Melody going to be a problem between us?' His tone was quiet yet firm.

'She could be. I've told you, Dave. I'm just not comfortable around children.'

'Why?'

'Because that's the way I am,' she replied forcefully.

'What happened?' He gazed into her eyes and she felt as though he were touching her soul. She shivered and crossed her arms in front. 'Tell me, Rosie.'

'I…I can't,' she whispered. 'It will upset me for the rest of the day and I…I can't afford to have that happen.'

He exhaled deeply and raked his fingers through his hair. 'I see.' He looked at his now empty plate. 'That was delicious. Thank you for allowing me to come over for breakfast.' He stood and carried his plate and utensils to the dishwasher and stacked them inside.

'You're leaving?'

He groaned softly. 'I don't know what to do, Rosie. I think perhaps it's best if I did leave, for the moment.'

'Why? Are you going to say something you might regret?'

'No. It's not that. In fact, I don't know what it is. That's the truth. We seem to be going around in circles. I want to be with you and I think you want to be with me—and I don't mean that in a physical sense.'

'Ah, so you don't think what's happening between us is just physical,' she stated.

'I've never met anyone like you before, Rosie.' He came to stand behind her and placed his hands on her shoulders, kneading gently. 'You're direct, straightforward, yet you can be as cool as an ice queen when it suits you.'

'Protection,' she murmured as she closed her eyes, not only enjoying the massage but his closeness as well.

'I know. We all have our barriers. Just like the echidna. We put up our spikes whenever we're being attacked.'

'What are your barriers, Dave? Am I going to be able to break through them?'

'Do you want to break through them?' he countered quietly.

'I...I don't know.' He stopped massaging but didn't remove his hands so the warmth was still spreading down her shoulders and flooding deep within her. Her blood pumped faster around her body; her pulse mimicked the pace. 'Things have just been happening too fast but, try as I might, I just can't seem to slow them down.'

He chuckled. 'Especially when I'm barging in here, inviting myself to breakfast.'

'Did you hear me strenuously objecting?'

'Did I give you time?' He bent his head and nuzzled her neck. 'You smell incredible.' He placed light kisses on her skin and Rose closed her eyes, letting her head rest back against him. She parted her lips as her breathing increased, savouring the sensations he was evoking deep within her. 'I'm having such a hard time keeping my hands off you, Rosie. Now, that's definitely physical.'

Rose swallowed. 'I know what you mean.' She turned in his arms to face him and, placing her hands on either side of his face, brought his lips down to meet her own. She sighed with longing as he moved his mouth over hers. This was the only time she felt complete. When she was with Dave and he was kissing her. Reality seemed suspended and she wished she could live in the moment for ever.

'Sweetheart,' he groaned a few minutes later as he eased back but didn't let her go. 'It's almost half past seven and I'm due at the hospital for ward round soon.'

Rose nodded. 'So where do we go from here, Dave?'

'I'm not sure, Rosie. We'll just have to figure it out as we go along.' He bent his head and kissed her quickly. 'Do you need help cleaning up here?'

'No. I'll put it all in the dishwasher with the dishes from last night and switch it on before I go.'

'When are you leaving?'

'In about two minutes. It's Wednesday—baby day.'

'How many C-sections are there this morning?' He took a few steps away and put his hands in his shorts pockets as though he was having a hard time keeping his hands off her.

'I think there's two.'

'All right. Well, you have fun. Are we still on for dinner tonight?'

'Sure.'

'We'll talk more then.' Still keeping his hands where they were, he leaned forward again and kissed her once more. 'Sorry,' he said with that lopsided grin that always melted her heart. 'I told you I find you irresistible.'

Rose laughed. 'Thanks for stopping by.'

'I'll see myself out.'

Rose turned her attention to the sink, determined to get to the hospital as soon as possible. The sooner she got this day under way, the sooner it would be time for dinner. Dinner with Dave.

CHAPTER NINE

THE rest of the day passed in a blur as Dave anxiously counted the minutes until he would be alone with Rosie again. He hadn't been lying when he'd told her she was addictive and the more he saw of her, the harder he felt himself falling.

'What's the matter with you?' Sadie quizzed as she showed in his last patient. 'You've been as jumpy as a red roo all day long.'

'Probably getting excited about seeing his little girl tomorrow,' the patient supplied.

'Good point,' Sadie remarked, and Dave thought it safer just to smile and let them think what they wanted.

'How old is she now, Dave?' his patient asked, and she wasn't the first one to have asked that question during the course of the day. He smiled politely and murmured the correct responses, all the while trying to squash his impatience for the day to be over.

Finally, the patient was finished and as he sat down to write up the notes he heard footsteps coming down the corridor. 'What now?' he grumbled quietly. The polite smile he'd pasted onto his face changed to one of relief and genuine surprise as Rosie walked into his room and sat down opposite him.

'What a day.' She sighed.

'I know what you mean. How are you holding up?' He finished writing and closed the case notes with finality. His clinic was done!

'Nothing a good night's sleep wouldn't fix, but I don't seem to be having many of them.'

'Ah, now, that's a lie. I know for a fact that you had a

decent sleep the night you got food poisoning—well, once you stopped vomiting.'

'Yuck!' Rose grimaced and covered her face with her hands. 'Don't remind me. I must have looked awful.'

Dave stood and came around the desk to crouch down beside her chair. 'You looked amazing.'

'Amazingly awful,' she said on a laugh.

'No. Amazingly stunning,' he whispered, and the mood between them instantly changed to one of sensual delight. Dave edged in closer and raised one hand to caress her cheek. When her eyelids fluttered closed at the slight contact, that was when his restraint snapped.

'I need to kiss you,' he whispered hoarsely, his tone deep with desire.

'Ditto,' she replied, and shifted so their impatient lips could meet. She sighed into his embrace and leaned a little too heavily towards him.

'Whoa. Whoa—hang on, I'm...' Tightening his grip around her, hoping it would steady him, Dave lost his balance completely and toppled backwards, bringing Rose with him. 'Ugh!' She landed on top of him, their legs sprawled and tangled together. She started to shake. 'Rosie?' No reply. 'Rosie? Are you all right?'

Rose lifted her head, tears streaming down her face.

'Where are you hurt?' he asked instantly, not sure whether he should move her off him or not.

Rose gasped for breath and that was when he realised she wasn't crying at all but laughing instead. He relaxed back onto the floor. 'Oh! The look on your face as you went was priceless,' she said between giggles. 'Thank you, I needed that.' And she reached up and kissed him on the lips.

'Oh, fair dinkum, Dave Dunbar,' Sadie spluttered from the doorway. 'Is *this* the girlie who's had you in a tailspin all day long?'

'Uh, *now* someone calls you by your surname!' Rose mumbled in his ear, which had him chuckling. She looked up, unable to believe they'd been caught in such a compromising position. Sadie glared down at both of them, especially at her. Slowly, they untangled themselves and stood on their feet.

'Really, Dave, I expected better of you. Besides, I thought you didn't like blondes.'

'Sadie.' His voice held a hint of warning. 'You may have known me since I was born but that doesn't mean you know what I like and don't like.'

'But *she* was a blonde.'

'Yes. You're correct. *Margaret* was a blonde and so is Rosie, but apart from hair colour they are nothing alike.'

'Fine.'

Rose thought Sadie was obviously smart enough to know when to pick fights with Dave and when not to. 'I came down to tell you that you're both needed for an emergency. Hazel Fredrick is being brought in with abdominal pains.'

'Let's go, then.' He reached for Rose's hand and together they walked out.

'She wasn't too happy, was she?' Rose risked a glance over her shoulder to find Sadie glaring at her.

'Do you think I really care what Sadie or anyone else in this town thinks of whom I choose to date?'

'Uh…I don't know. Do you?'

He opened the door to the stairwell and waited for her to go first. 'No.' Their footsteps echoed as they headed down to A and E. 'Who I choose to spend time with is my business and no one else's.'

'Glad to hear it. Julian was always more concerned about what other people thought.' She went to pull open the door that led to A and E but he stopped her. He leaned in close, one hand still up against the door.

'I'm not Julian.' His tone was firm and Rose nodded. Dave bent his head and claimed her lips, his kiss more possessive than before. When he pulled back, he took her hand in his, opened the door and led her through the A and E department. People's heads turned and whispers broke out as he led her to the tearoom.

'I figured it was OK to hold your hand in public now,' he stated with a crooked smile. 'No doubt Sadie had already phoned her juicy bit of gossip around the hospital before we reached the bottom of the stairwell.'

'No doubt.' Rose shrugged. 'Nothing to be done about it now.'

'So much for trying to save your reputation.'

She smiled tiredly back at him. 'So much for dinner,' she said.

'You're right,' he groaned. 'At least you understand.'

'I'm not Margaret.'

'Touché!' Dave laughed. They heard the ambulance sirens and headed out to triage. 'Good evening, Mrs Fredrick,' he said as she was wheeled in to treatment room two. 'I gather you're not feeling the best.'

'Can't say I am, Dave.'

'Tell me where it hurts.'

While Dave examined Mrs Fredrick, Rose checked the ambulance notes to see what pain relief she'd already been given.

'I'd like to do an ultrasound,' Dave told his patient once he'd finished examining her. 'I think it might be gallstones and the ultrasound will confirm it.'

'Do I need an operation?' Mrs Fredrick asked, her tone worried.

'Hopefully not. Nowadays, we use a technique called lithotripsy. It's where ultrasonic shock waves shatter the stones. Once that's done, they'll be passed naturally into the bile duct and then the bowel. First of all, though, let's confirm that it is gallstones which are giving you this pain.'

Dave's diagnosis turned out to be spot on and once Mrs Fredrick's treatment had been completed, they left her to rest. Rose ensured she had sufficient medication authorised to get her through the night.

'Now we just wait and see if the stones pass by themselves. I'll be surprised if they don't.' Dave placed his arm about her shoulders as they walked out to the car park. 'Hungry?'

'Surprisingly not, but if you want something, I guess I can make us a bite of dinner.'

'I don't expect you to cook for me,' he told her as they came to stand by her car.

'I'm like my dad. Cooking relaxes me.'

'Well, in that case...' He laughed and gathered her closer, noticing the tired lines around her eyes. 'Actually, sweetheart, it's getting late and I've got a busy day tomorrow, getting things ready for when Mel and the nanny arrive.'

'Oh, yeah. That's tomorrow.' The smile disappeared from her face and her voice became flat. Why did everything have to become so complicated? It didn't matter how hard she worked to block out the fact that Dave had a daughter, it never quite worked. Reality had a way of intruding.

'Do you ever want to have any?' He kept his eyes focused on hers.

Rose swallowed nervously. 'Children?'

He nodded.

'Truthfully, Dave...I don't know.'

'I see.'

'Do you? Everything's just happened so fast, Dave. You only really kissed me properly last night. Then you tell me you have a child, and not only that but she's coming to live with you. The next bombshell was that my ex-fiancé is marrying your ex-wife. That's quite a lot to deal with in such a short space of time.'

'I know, Rosie.' He kissed her forehead and held her tight. They stood like that for a few minutes before Rose edged away.

'I don't like being rushed and right now that's exactly how I feel. Julian rushed me and it ended in pain—and before you say anything,' she continued when he opened his mouth, 'I know you're not Julian. You're very different from him. You're caring and considerate and chivalrous and…and extremely sexy, but it's as though you need to get our relationship, whatever that may be, onto a more even footing before your daughter arrives tomorrow.' She took a breath. 'I'm sorry, Dave, but I just don't feel it's possible. You're going to need to spend time with Melody when she arrives to make her feel more comfortable with the changes happening in her life. I understand this so I think, perhaps, that we should just…you know, cool it for a while.'

He was silent for a few minutes and she wondered whether she'd lost even a remote chance of a relationship with him. 'Dave,' she said softly, 'I didn't mean to go on like that. I'm telling you how I feel. I'm being honest. Isn't that what you wanted?'

'Yes.' He nodded. 'It's just not as easy to deal with as I'd anticipated.'

'What? Me not being completely comfortable with things?'

'No. A woman who actually communicates.'

She smiled. 'I could say the same about you.'

'I've heard what you've said, Rosie, and I respect it, but I can't stop seeing you. I'm at the stage that if I *don't* see you, I feel like I'm going to go insane. You're right about Mel, though. I do need to spend time with her but there's no reason why the three of us couldn't do it together.' He felt her tense beneath his arms but went on. 'I'm going to move from the farm and get a place in town. I've already looked at a few places but wanted Mel to help choose. After all, she'll be living there, too.'

'What about the papers—from Margaret?'

'They came this morning. My solicitor's looked at them and it appears everything is going to go through uncontested and smoothly. With Mags getting married on Saturday and then leaving the country, things are moving like the proverbial freight train, but there's nothing else to do.'

Dave raised her chin slowly until their gazes met. 'I need to be with you, Rosie.' He placed a kiss on her lips. 'You're very special to me.' He kissed her again. 'I know this has been incredibly fast but…' he shrugged '…it's just the way things have turned out.' He kissed her once more before leaning his forehead against hers.

'I know Julian probably belittled your existence but don't believe anything that creep said. Cutting people down is the only way he can make himself look big. I've seen him do it, Rosie, and you're way beyond him. Believe me when I say you're a lovely person—inside and out. I've seen you with patients, I've seen you overcome your fears. You're strong and independent. It may not feel that way but you are. You took the chance to come here to Broken Hill, to give yourself a fresh start and to spend more time with your father. That tells me so much about the real you, Rosie.

This time, when he kissed her, it was slow and sensual, making her feel as though she were floating on a cloud. With the utmost certainty, his mouth moved over hers, his tongue tracing the outline of her lips before slipping between them.

His touch remained gentle yet provocative. Sweet yet electrifying. She may have been floating but desire exploded deep within her. His hands were drawing little circles on her back, causing floods of tingles to spread in every direction. Her heart was pounding fiercely against her ribs and she was positive he could hear it. She moaned with delight, threading her fingers through his hair.

Dave nearly crumbled completely as her fingers plunged through his hair, ensuring his head was kept firmly in place. The spiralling passion that he could feel building to a frenzy was becoming harder to control with every passing second. What was it about this woman and her completely uninhibited response to him? She was a natural aphrodisiac and one he was finding he couldn't get enough of. He pressed his body hard up against hers, pressing her back against her car. Her car!

Dave pulled back suddenly and looked around them.

'What's wrong?' Rosie's tone was a mixture of desire and confusion.

'Sorry, sweetheart. I just remembered where we were.' His wry grin was crooked and she felt her heart melt once more.

'I see your point,' she said, drawing in a deep breath. 'Kissing in the car park like a couple of adolescent teenagers.'

'Guess we'd better get going,' he replied, not moving away from her.

'Guess we'd better.'

'You have a really good sleep tonight. Doctor's orders. OK?'

'Why? Do I look all drawn and ugly?'

He chuckled. 'Would you believe me if I said no?' He kissed her lips again. 'You know you look beautiful, Rosie, and if you don't, take my word for it because it's true.'

She smiled. 'I guess I'll have to.'

'Here. Let me open your door for you.'

'Always the gentleman.'

'Chivalry, remember.'

'How could I forget? You and your brother seem to have it in spades. Someone in your upbringing did something right.'

'Yeah. I guess they did. Never thought of it that way before.' He kissed her again. 'Sleep sweet, Rosie—and I mean it.'

She laughed. 'I promise to do my best but with memories of kisses like the ones we've just shared, I don't know whether they're going to relax me or keep me awake!' She raised her eyebrows suggestively and laughed again when Dave groaned.

'Don't torture me. I'll call you.'

'I'd like that.'

She stepped forward and, reaching up, pressed her lips to his. 'Get in the car,' he growled. Rose smiled, glad to know she had the same encompassing effect on him as he had on her.

Finally, she pulled out of the car park and headed back to her father's house. As she drove, she thought about what they'd said tonight and was pleased with their progress. Even though she wanted to slow things down, she'd been happy to hear that Dave didn't know if he could.

He was everything she'd been looking for in a man and the thought scared the life out of her. He had a child and, although she'd come to terms with that, she still wasn't quite sure how she felt about it. 'All you need to do is to relax and be honest with them.' Rose repeated Dave's words out loud. *Was* it that easy?

Was Dave worth taking the chance on? Rose shook her head as she pulled into her father's driveway. 'Sleep?' she queried as she walked to her room. 'Ha!'

Rose dragged herself from the depths of sleep as the phone persisted in ringing. Maybe it was Dave? He'd said he'd call her. She flicked the covers back and stumbled out of bed, stubbing her toe on the wall as she rounded a corner to silence the offending instrument.

'Ow! Yes? What?'

'Rosie? Are you all right?'

'Oh, hi, Dad.' She tried to keep the disappointment from her tone. 'Yes, I'm fine. I just stubbed my toe, getting to the phone.'

'Did I wake you? Don't tell me I've got the time difference mixed up again. I thought it was about seven-thirty.'

Was it? Rose glanced at the grandfather clock that stood in the hall. 'Oh, no!' she gasped.

'What now?'

'Nothing. No, you didn't get the time wrong, Dad. I've

just slept in, that's all.' She bent down and examined her toe more closely, wincing slightly from her own light touch. It was fine.

'Really? That's not like you.'

'No,' she agreed as she realised it had been the first *really* good sleep she'd had since she'd arrived here. She took a deep breath and let it out slowly. 'Everything OK in honeymoon paradise?'

'Actually, no.'

'Dad? What's happened?' Rose was instantly alert.

'Oh, we're both fine, dear. It's the weather. It's turned bad and hasn't stopped raining. You know how unpredictable tropical weather can be at this time of year.'

'Sure. So you're coming home early?'

'Yes. We'll be back tomorrow. No point in hanging around as we were due to leave on Saturday so it's only a day early. Besides, Bev's missing everyone so we'll be back tomorrow.'

'Do you need me to pick you up from the airport?'

'No. We'll find our own way home. Well, you'd better run, princess, if you're going to make it to the hospital on time.'

'You're right. OK. See you tomorrow, Dad. Love you. Bye.' The instant she'd replaced the receiver, Rose hobbled back to her bedroom and quickly dug out some clothes. After showering and quickly drinking a glass of orange juice, she headed out the door. By the time she got to the hospital, Dave was ready to start his list.

'Sorry,' she mumbled, as she raced in and quickly changed into theatre garb. They had no time together and although she felt a little deflated, she was glad to at least be in the same room as him. Their gazes met a few times across the busy theatre and she saw the repressed desire that she knew was mirrored in her own.

Every patient she met that day, every nurse she spoke to, interns, theatre staff—everyone—gave her knowing little glances or big beaming smiles, except for Sadie who scowled at her instead. At lunch, she was sitting in the cafeteria, sipping a cup of tea, when Dave walked in. He smiled and waved at her and it was then she realised that a hush had fallen over the place.

Dave slowed his pace and stopped by her chair. 'Fine,' he said to the room. 'The rumours are true. Rosie and I are dating so now that the announcement is out of the way, would you, please, leave us alone?'

A few people clapped, others just started talking to the person next to them, but once more the place was filled with noise. 'Whew!' he said as he sat down beside her, giving her a quick peck on the lips. 'It's been a long time since I've been gossiped about.'

Rose laughed. 'Serves you right. You should have gone to greater lengths to protect my reputation. How's Mrs Fredrick this morning? She looked good when I saw her earlier but what's your professional opinion?'

'Lithotripsy appears to have been successful.'

'Excellent.' They ate lunch together then Rose's pager sounded.

'Ah. Looks as though the ophthalmology surgeon is ready to begin. I'd better go.'

Dave leaned over and kissed her again. 'How do you like being under the microscope?' he asked with a grin.

'Not very much, but I guess I'll just have to put up with it—especially after your little announcement,' she teased. 'I'll speak to you later.' With that, she left. Dave watched her go, his feelings for her increasing with every passing second.

He was really falling for her—in a big way—and he was determined to enjoy every minute of it.

'Hi, gorgeous,' Dave said, as he strode towards his daughter. She was coming out of the small aircraft which had finally come to a stop a few minutes ago.

'Hi, Dad,' she said, heaving a bag into her hand, her teddy bear tucked securely beneath her other arm. It was the bear he'd given her when he'd first seen her, and he was delighted that it was her favourite toy.

He gave her a quick hug, noting she didn't sound or look too happy. Dave glanced around. 'Where's the nanny?'

'She didn't come,' Melody told him matter-of-factly, although he thought he saw her bottom lip quiver.

'What?' Dave exploded, and went up the steps of the small plane to check for himself. It was empty. He looked down at Melody before coming to stand before her. He noticed she looked very worried and he quickly crouched down in front of her, bringing himself to her height. 'Have you travelled all this way by yourself?' he asked gently.

Melody's lower lip began to wobble. 'Yes.' Her eyes filled with tears and Dave found his own doing the same.

'Oh, baby.' He reached for her and brought her safely into his arms. Melody dropped the bag she was holding and buried her face into his chest. Dave held her protectively, knowing this was one female he would *always* be protective about—as was his right! 'Shh, princess. It's all right. Daddy's here.' He couldn't *believe* Margaret had done this! To let a six-year-old travel all that way by herself.

Of course, the flight attendants would have looked after her but still—how horrible. No child should ever have to go through that and he'd be damned if his daughter was ever going through something like that again.

Dave clenched his jaw in anger at his ex-wife. Thank goodness she'd signed the custody form. Now Melody was *his* daughter and he was going to protect her in any way he could, and if that meant keeping her away from her own natural mother, that's the way it would be.

'Mummy said I had to be brave. That I was a big girl now and didn't need a nanny,' Melody sobbed.

'Shh. It's all right, princess. It's all right. Daddy's here. I'll fix it,' he crooned, and stroked her long blonde hair. Slowly, her tears subsided and she stood back from him, automatically smoothing down her designer outfit. She held herself aloof, just like Mags had always done after an emotional outburst, and Dave realised he had his work cut out for him. Poor Melody didn't know how to behave any differently.

'Feeling a bit hot?'

'Yes.' She wiped at her blue eyes and nodded.

'Let's get you home and into some play clothes, eh?'

'I don't have any play clothes. Besides, my nanny—that is, my old nanny—gave me lots of school work to get done. She told me that you'd be out most of the time and that I'd have to be by myself so I may as well do some work.'

Dave looked at his daughter with incredulity. He'd never heard such nonsense but now was not the time or the place for such discussions. He shook his head slowly and bent to pick up her bag. 'Where are the rest of your bags, princess?'

Her bottom lip was still quivering as she shook her head.

'This is all there is?'

'Mummy said I wouldn't need many things out here. She gave the rest of my things away.' The tears were flowing again and Dave hoisted her up into his arms, holding her tightly as she cried yet again. The mental traumas this child had been through, and all because of her self-righteous mother. His heart melted when her own little arms came around his neck, holding him tight. He dropped the bag and stroked her hair back from her face as she cried.

'Need a hand?' one of the ladies from the air terminal asked quietly, and Dave nodded. He carried Melody to his ute. 'Come on, princess. Let's get you home.'

'It's…not…my…home.' She hiccuped between the words. 'I…don't…have one and I'm *not* a princess.'

Dave clipped her seat belt around her and rubbed his fingers gently down her cheek. 'You are a princess,

Melody. You're *my* princess and Daddy's never going to let anyone hurt you again.'

'But…but…you don't like…me.'

She couldn't have inflicted any more damage on his heart if she'd pierced it with a sword. 'What? Melody—*I love you.*'

'But…but…Mummy said you…didn't…like me and that's why…you wouldn't come and get…me.'

Dave kissed her head, holding her as she cried again. She was obviously very tired and she'd had such a terrible and emotionally draining day that he couldn't blame her for the constant tears and outbursts. He clenched his jaw again, unable to believe that Mags had said such things to her daughter. He should have flown to Sydney and collected Mel. He should have followed his gut instinct and now he was furious with himself. Why had he listened to that witch?

He took a deep breath. 'You're wrong, Melody. Mummy was wrong.' Dave could feel tears pricking at his own eyes as he gazed down at her tear-stained face. 'I *love* you, *so* much.' A tear dropped from his lashes. 'You're my precious girl and you're very, *very* special to me.' He wanted to tell her that they'd never be apart again, but he wasn't sure what else Mags had told her. He wanted to say she could rely on him for the truth and that he'd do everything he could to be a good father—but he knew it would be too much, too soon.

'Little steps,' he whispered, as he wiped her tears again. 'We'll take little steps in our new life together.'

Melody looked up at him, nodded and sniffled, her bottom lip still protruding slightly. She reached out her little hand and gently wiped away his own tears. The tender action caused the lump in his throat to swell, and his heart filled with pride at her gentleness.

There was hope.

He knew it.

He felt it.

CHAPTER TEN

ROSE wasn't surprised that she didn't hear from Dave on Thursday night as he was probably spending time with Melody. She had to face facts. There was another woman in his life now, and even though she was only six, it meant that his time would be divided between them.

She frowned. Surely she wasn't jealous of a six-year-old! From what Dave had told her, and how she knew Julian would have treated the child, Melody had obviously been through the wringer lately. Now she had to adjust to a new life here in Broken Hill with her father—but what part was Rose supposed to play?

She paced around the house once more, unable to control her thoughts. She knew she could call him. That in this day and age it was fine for women to give men a call, especially when they were dating, but she couldn't do it. She was still very uncertain about herself, thanks to Julian and the degrading way he had constantly put doubt into her mind. She could almost hear him now.

'Do you think that would be the right thing to do, Rose? Imposing on people like that? It's very rude—at least I think it's rude.'

Comments such as that had been made constantly throughout her time with him, and she wondered why she hadn't realised it had just been his way of manipulating her. How had she been so stupid?

Cross with herself, and determined not to let her silly neuroses get in the way, she took out her address book, checked Dave's number and picked up the phone. When she got to the last digit, she hung up again.

'I can't do it,' she said as she paced around the kitchen.

'Yes, you can,' she retorted, and headed back to the phone. She dialled again, forcing herself to take a deep breath and relax. She was anxious to hear his voice. Anxious to feel those tiny tingles that flooded her body when he spoke to her. Anxious to know he was nearby and thinking of her.

'Yes?' His tone was brisk.

'Dave?' Rose asked hesitantly, checking the number in her address book again. Had she dialled wrong?

'Rosie.' His voice softened marginally. 'What can I do for you?'

'Uh…' Now what? Oh, she was no good at this. 'I…uh…just wanted to see how things went. How did things go with Melody and the nanny?' She hoped the nanny was a middle-aged woman with warts on her face, rather than the red-headed beauty she'd been imagining.

'Fine.'

'Is something wrong?'

'Melody's about to go to bed but she doesn't want to sleep in the spare room. I told her she could sleep out here on the couch, but it really isn't that comfortable.'

'Um…well, why don't you let her sleep with you to-night?' she ventured. 'Surely it couldn't hurt. Just for to-night. The first night in a strange place is always uncomfortable.'

'Yeah.' He relaxed a little. 'Good thinking. She's had a terrible time of it, poor kid.' He lowered his voice to a whisper. 'The nanny didn't come. Mel came the entire way from Sydney by herself.'

'What? What happened to the nanny?' Rose asked in stunned disbelief. Her insides twisted in horror at the thought of a six-year-old girl travelling all that way by herself.

'Mags said she didn't need a nanny.' Dave's tone was harsh and Rose didn't blame him.

'What are you going to do about tomorrow? You've got house calls and a clinic.'

He groaned. 'I'd forgotten. I have no idea.'

'What about Mick? Or his girlfriend?'

'He and his girlfriend are leaving for Adelaide in the morning. They can't cancel the trip or postpone it. They won't be back until early Saturday morning.'

'I see.' Rose thought quickly, unable to believe what she was about to do. Her heart was hammering wildly against her ribs and her throat went dry. 'Well, I'm…um…not due in Theatre—at least for tomorrow morning.' She had planned to get through some paperwork but it could always wait. Rose knew from experience that no child should ever be made to feel unwanted. 'I have a list in the afternoon, though.'

'Are you sure?' He sounded cautious. 'I appreciate the offer but if it's going to make you uncomfortable then I can make alternate arrangements.'

'I…er…want to do this, Dave. I want to help you out.' She wasn't at all sure but the caring note in his voice had helped override the fear she was starting to experience. 'Just relax and be honest, right?'

His laugh was incredulous. She'd remembered what he'd said and was willing to apply it. 'That's right. You're one remarkable woman, Rosie Partridge.'

'Thanks,' she said softly. 'Do you want me to come out to the farm?'

'Actually, I think she might appreciate getting away from the farm. It's not a great place for a kid to stay.' He looked over at his daughter, sitting primly on one of the old, uncomfortable chairs, clutching her teddy to her for dear life. She looked frightened—scared—and he wondered if she was listening to his conversation. He raked his free hand through his hair. 'I'll drop her off tomorrow morning. Right now, I'd better go.'

'All right. See you in the morning.'

'Bye.' He hung up the phone and went over to Melody. 'How about sleeping in Daddy's big bed tonight?'

'With you?' Her eyes widened as she looked at him and

for a moment he felt as though she were reaching right into his soul.

'Do you want to?' he asked slowly, and was pleased with her emphatic nod.

'I remember doing that the last time I was here and it was fun.'

Dave smiled at the way she'd instantly brightened. 'Good. Off you go, then. Get into my bed.'

He waited for her to get beneath the thin cotton sheet, the gentle whirring of the ceiling fan above them. He sat on the other side of the bed and lifted his legs on top of the sheet after kicking off his shoes. Melody shifted over and snuggled into him. Dave ran his fingers gently through her hair, his gut twisting with an overpowering and protective love.

'Daddy's got to go to work in the morning,' he said softly. 'And Uncle Mick has to go on a trip to Adelaide for the day.'

'But—'

'Shh,' he whispered. 'Just listen for a moment. I want to introduce you to…a friend of mine. Her name is Rosie and she's a doctor, just like me. We work together at the hospital but she doesn't need to come to the hospital tomorrow morning and she asked if you could go to her house to play.'

'Play?'

'Yes.' Dave wasn't sure how Rosie would cope with playing with a six-year-old but he didn't want Melody to feel unwanted. Besides, Rosie *had* offered. 'So that will be exciting, won't it?'

'I guess,' Melody replied, yawning once again.

Dave bent his head and kissed the top of hers. 'All right, princess. Time to go to sleep, and don't hog the bed like you did last time.'

Melody giggled before yawning again. 'What does "hog the bed" mean?'

'It means you take up all the room,' he explained. 'Now

shush and close your eyes.' He continued to stroke her hair, letting his thoughts wander. How would Rosie and Melody cope tomorrow? The importance of the situation penetrated him. Rosie was everything he'd ever wanted in a woman. She was intelligent, lively, spirited, direct and most of all honest. He loved the way they argued, the way she knew it was just an argument and didn't take it too seriously. He loved the way she deftly raised her chin and squared her shoulders when she was preparing to give him a piece of her mind. He smiled at the memory. They were both hotheads with tempers that sparked easily and cooled just as quickly.

They had so much in common and tomorrow he'd introduce her to the other important female in his life—his daughter. He ignored the instinct that told him it might not be as easy as he hoped.

But surely when Rosie met Melody—in person—things would be different... Wouldn't they? He knew she'd been burnt by Julian and his indifferent treatment of his own children, but *he* wasn't like that. He loved his daughter and wanted her with him.

He stopped moving his hand on Melody's hair as realisation struck. Was that it? Did Rosie want to be the only woman in his life? He'd asked her if she'd wanted children and she'd said she didn't know. What did that mean? Didn't *most* women want children?

He glanced down at his daughter who, he realised, was now asleep. His heart swelled with paternal love. How could anyone not want children? They were so...amazing. So fantastic. So humbling.

'It has to be her own childhood,' he murmured, as he carefully slid out of Melody's grasp. He walked through to the kitchen and took a beer out of the fridge. He cracked it open and took a long drink. 'What happened to her mother?'

'Talking to yourself again, bro'?' Mick asked as he walked into the room.

'Something like that.' Dave headed out to the verandah. Mick followed, sipping on a beer as well.

'Problems with Rosie?'

'Ha! When aren't there problems with women?'

'Want to talk about it?'

'She's just so…different. I'm in love with her, Mick.'

'Tell me something I *don't* know.'

'How could you know? I've only just realised it myself.'

'Hello! I live with you, remember? You've been different ever since she arrived in town. You've fallen faster than a lead balloon, and so has she. What's the problem?'

'You think Rosie loves me?' Dave couldn't help the smile of pride that filled him.

'Sure. A blind man could see that. As I said, what's the problem?'

'She doesn't like kids.'

'Are you for real?'

'Yes.'

'How do you know?'

'I asked her.' He drained his drink and leant against the verandah rail. 'I want more kids, Mick. I don't want Melody to be an only child and I want to be there from the beginning, to feel my child kick inside Rosie.'

'So she doesn't want to have kids?'

'She's not sure.' He exhaled sharply and looked up at the star-filled night. 'I've got so many unanswered questions, Mick.'

'Then why don't you find out what the answers are?'

Dave stared at his brother. 'You're right. What's the time?'

'Just after nine.'

'Look after Melody, for me, mate.' Dave stalked into the kitchen and returned a moment later with his car keys. 'I need to speak to Rosie.'

'Maybe you should call first.'

'You know me,' Dave replied as he opened the car door. 'Spontaneity at its best!'

* * *

Rose rested her head back on the edge of the bath, determined to get rid of her headache. This was her last night of peace and quiet and she was going to enjoy it with a relaxing soak. The water was like satin against her skin and the scented bubbles were enough to make her drowsy.

She refused to let herself think about the multitude of problems floating around in her head. Tonight she was going to relax and pamper herself a little. She'd taken the phone off the hook and turned out all the lights. The gentle breeze from the bathroom window ensured she didn't get too hot and the five beautiful, flickering candles gave the room a soft glow. She closed her eyes, taking her first deep relaxing breath in days.

Her worries started to slip away, which was what baths like that were designed to do. As she continued to lie there, her mind turned to Dave. She blocked out any unanswered questions she might have and just focused on how much she cared about him. He'd become so special to her in such a short time. What she'd told him about not being rushed had been absolutely true, yet in some ways it was thrilling to be so caught up with emotions the way she'd been since arriving in Broken Hill—emotions that Dave alone was responsible for.

She thought about how gorgeous he'd looked when she'd seen him arm-wrestling in the pub. Had he really been ogling her back then? Little flutterings of excitement sprang to life in her stomach as she realised he had, especially if his kisses were anything to go by.

The way his mouth felt when it met hers…it was as though they'd been designed for each other. Never had she experienced emotions of this magnitude before but, then, she'd never been in love—*really* in love—with a man.

Oh, she'd told herself she'd been in love with Julian but it was nothing compared to how she felt for Dave. She could yell at Dave. She could lose her temper. She could be at her worst and he still found her attractive. It was as though he knew she had faults and simply accepted them, rather than trying to change her.

Rose sighed as her love for him grew once more. She allowed her imagination to run wild. She and Dave were married and this was their house. After a hectic day at the hospital they'd come home together, and when it was his turn to cook he'd draw her a scented bath and tell her to unwind, bringing her in a cool glass of wine, desire sparking in his eyes. He wouldn't disturb her, though, because he'd be able to tell she just needed some time by herself.

After dinner, they'd make love, giving everything to each other. Not holding anything back. The image of Dave, lying with his legs entwined with hers, their bodies covered with the afterglow of spent passion, made her heart swell with happiness.

'Rosie?' The knock at the front door startled her from her dreams, and she realised she'd almost fallen asleep. The house was quiet and for a second she thought she'd imagined it. She'd been so caught up in her fantasies of Dave that she'd thought for a second he was here.

'Rosie?'

She hadn't imagined it. What did she do now? Her heart began to race. Why was he here? Should she pretend she was asleep or answer the door?

'Rosie?' His voice was fainter and she realised he was walking around to the back door. Then she remembered he knew where the spare key was hidden. He'd used it to get into the house the night she'd had food poisoning. Moments later she heard footsteps coming hesitantly through the house. 'Rosie? It's Dave. Is everything all right?'

If she didn't move soon, he'd be walking in to find her in the bath, yet she found herself unable to move a muscle. Her heart was drumming so loudly, the noise was reverberating in her ears. She swallowed, amazed to find her mouth suddenly dry.

'Rosie!'

It was the urgency in his tone that helped her to respond. The last thing she wanted was to worry him. 'Just a minute,' she called back as loudly as she could. The footsteps stopped, just outside her open bedroom door. The door to the *en suite* bathroom was open as well. A few more footsteps followed, but these were muffled by the carpet on the floor.

She watched as he materialised in the doorway.

'U-uh…' He faltered, stunned to find her relaxing in a bubble bath, lit only by the glow of some candles. His mouth opened at the sight of her and his eyes filled with desire. Rose swallowed, once more unable to move. They just stared at each other, the silent messages being interpreted fluently.

Dave instantly regretted not taking Mick's advice and calling before he'd just turned up on her doorstep. All rational thought disappeared from his mind as he just stared at her lying there, surrounded by white, glistening bubbles.

'If you don't mind…waiting outside my bedroom…I'll get out.' Rose was surprised to find her voice so husky but there was nothing she could do about it.

'U-uh…sure.' His legs felt as though they weighed a ton as he went out of her bedroom, closing the door behind him.

She moved in the bath, not at all surprised to discover her arms were shaky. She quickly towelled herself dry and wrapped herself up in a big bathrobe. 'All right. You can come in now.' She fiddled nervously with the end of the sash that held her robe in place.

When he opened the door, her breath caught in her throat. Oh, he was gorgeous, and she had the urge to let her fingers memorise the contours of his body in great detail.

With a few short strides, he'd crossed the room and gathered her into his arms. His mouth on hers was hot and demanding. Not that she minded. Given the direction her own thoughts had taken, it seemed appropriate he was here.

'Rosie.' Her name escaped his lips as they momentarily gasped for breath. Dave plundered her mouth, his tongue seeking and receiving a response. How did this woman do it? She had the ability to knock him beyond the black stump with one simple look. Add to that the fact that whatever scent had been in the bath water now emanated from her skin, making him lose what vestige of control he had left.

'Rosie.' He smothered her neck with tiny kisses, unable to get enough of her. 'Rosie,' he murmured again, 'I love you.'

The words were like a dousing of cold water. Rose lifted her head away from him. 'You…you…what?'

'I love you,' he repeated again, his voice filled with desire. He gazed down into her eyes, knowing that what he was about to say could be a mistake but needing to say it anyway. 'I want to marry you, Rosie.'

'Marry!' The vision she'd had of this being *their* house ran through her mind again. She brushed it away. There were still so many issues they needed to resolve—the first one being his daughter!

He'd been right. He didn't stop her as she pulled away and took a few steps backwards. 'Look, I know I'm rushing you—'

'Rushing? You give the word new meaning, David.' She was shaking all over and she wasn't quite sure what from. Was it surprise? Disbelief or rage? All of those emotions and many more were coursing through her at a rate of knots, and her earlier tranquillity had been completely shattered. The knowledge that he loved her had come as a complete shock. She hadn't expected him to feel the same way about her as she did about him. Now…now he wanted to get married?

'Why shouldn't we get married? I love you, Rosie, and

I'm sure you feel the same way.' He paused for a second. 'Don't you?'

'Dave…' Rose stopped, throwing her arms up in confusion. 'Marriage?'

'What? What's so wrong with that?' He could see her withdrawing from him and knew he'd lost her—this time. He was a man with a mission and stubborn determination to boot. He knew with an absolute certainty that he wanted to marry Rosie Partridge. 'Is it Melody?'

'Well…yes…amongst other things.'

There was that honesty—slapping him in the face again. He narrowed his gaze, determined to get to the heart of the matter. 'What happened with your mother, Rosie? Why is it that you're so afraid of children?' He watched as she straightened her spine and raised her chin, defiance gleaming in her eyes. Didn't she know she looked irresistible when she did that?

'I'm not *afraid* of them… I've just never had much to do with children, that's all. Other than treating them in my paediatric rotation, that is,' she added as an afterthought.

'What happened with your mother?' he asked again, insistently.

'She left us,' Rose blurted out. 'When I was three.'

'Do you remember her at all?'

'No, but my father has told me all about her. She wasn't at all maternal.'

'Ah, and you think you're the same.'

'Well, the children I *have* met have never taken an instant liking to me so, yes, I guess so.'

'Yet you've just told me that you haven't had too many dealings with children.'

'And now you know why.' Rose rubbed her fingers along her forehead, feeling her earlier headache returning. 'I'd really like to get to bed early tonight, Dave.'

'Kicking me out, sweetheart? Not just yet.' His gaze roved over her again. 'Put some clothes on and I'll make us a cuppa.'

'Dave, I'd really prefer that you—'

'I'll make the tea,' he said more forcefully. 'We're going to talk about this, Rosie.'

'No, we're not. You can't just come waltzing in here, laying down the law. I'm tired, Dave, and I want to go to sleep.'

'I need to know.' He stood his ground, not moving an inch.

'What? You need to know that I look *exactly* like my mother? That I'm like her in so many ways it isn't funny? I'm not maternal, Dave. When I see children, I don't feel anything for them, except a need that they grow up.'

'That's not true.'

'How would you know? You're not me.' Her eyes radiated pure disbelief at his words. 'My mother was a bad mother and I'll probably end up being just like her. She wanted a career and hated being stuck at home with a child. I'm very career-minded—just like her. I love my job. I enjoy it and I don't want to give it up.'

'No one's asking you to.'

She shook her head. 'There's more to it than that. You wanted to know why I have mild claustrophobia, so I'll tell you. At least once a week she used to lock me in my room for most of the day. It was a very small room, even for a child.' Rose's words broke on a sob. 'She sometimes even left the house, leaving me in there with only a bottle of water. She was no good with children. She didn't know how to deal with the ordinary tantrums children have, the way they expand their boundaries.

'I may not remember these things but my father has always been honest with me and answered my questions when I asked. The mild claustrophobia wasn't discovered until recently and although I'm slowly getting better, it's going to take more time.' Rose could feel the hot, angry tears pricking at her eyes.

'I have *no* idea how to deal with children but I'll tell you this. I won't allow myself to lose control the way my mother did but I can't say for certain until I put myself in that situation. Don't you see? I can't trust *myself*. To think of the permanent psychological damage that's happened to me…' She shook her head emphatically. 'I won't do that to another child. I won't do it, Dave. I won't!' The tears were now streaming down her face and she knew she'd shocked him with her outburst.

He took a few steps towards her but she held up her hands to stop him. 'Don't. Don't touch me.'

'All right. I won't.' She could hear the love in his voice when he spoke, and it only tore through her with more pain than she thought she could bear. 'But I want you to at least listen.' His eyes were filled with understanding. 'You're not like your mother, Rosie. Believe me, you're not.'

'How would you know? You've never met her. You know nothing about her, except for what I've told you.'

'Sweetheart, you *care* about kids, otherwise you wouldn't be so conscious of what your mother did and how wrong it was. You've said you don't want to inflict permanent psychological damage on a child and *that*, in itself, is proof enough that you're nothing like your mother.'

She wanted to believe him. Oh, how she desperately wanted to believe him. She brushed back the tears with an impatient hand. 'Still, what if I crack? What if I can't cope and I'm horrible…?' Her voice caught on a sob. 'I just don't know, Dave. I'm not sure.' She shook her head.

'Then why did you offer to have Melody tomorrow?'

'Because of you.'

'See? You care.'

'About *you*, Dave.'

His heart nurtured that gem. 'That's a start.' He took another step closer but she held her hands up again. He stopped. She was behaving like a caged animal and in a way he could understand it. She was fenced in by the past and now that the door was open, she wasn't sure she wanted to step through it.

'You care about me, Rosie. Doesn't that show you how different you are to your mother? She obviously didn't care about your father or she would have stayed to work things out. She would have told him that she couldn't cope all day with a child and that she wanted a career, but she didn't. You're different.'

He edged closer but she simply edged back. 'You're open, honest. You communicate.' He smiled at her, that gorgeous crooked smile that always had the ability to melt her insides. 'You sure surprised me. A female who communicates.' He was moving slowly as he talked. 'I know you offered to have Melody tomorrow because you wanted to help me out, and you have no idea how much I appreciate that.' He reached out a hand to her. 'But I would never leave Mel with you if I didn't trust you one hundred per cent.'

'Get back,' she sobbed, as she felt the wall behind her. 'Please, just go.'

'Sweetheart, I'm not going to leave you in this state.'

'Yes, you are,' she responded forcefully. 'I've listened to what you've said and now I'd like you to go.' She sniffed and wished she had a handkerchief or tissue.

Dave stood his ground, unsure whether or not to leave her. She was in such an emotional turmoil that he didn't want her to spend the rest of the night sobbing out old memories that he'd obviously triggered.

'I feel responsible.' His voice was soft but he didn't move any closer. 'I'm glad things are out in the open, Rosie. Now we can move forward.' He held her gaze for a moment before acceding. 'I'll go but only because that's what you want.' He turned and headed to the door.

Rose held her breath, not sure whether she really wanted him to go. He stopped at the door and turned to look at her.

'The other thing you need to realise is that your mother

wasn't just bad at being a parent. Rosie, what she did to you was child abuse and neglect, and I'm sure your father has spent the rest of his life feeling guilty that he didn't do something to stop it sooner.

'Take the step, sweetheart. Step into the unknown.' He smiled at her. 'I'll be there to support you all the way and catch you if you start to fall.' He blew her a kiss before walking out. 'I'll lock the door behind me,' he called.

Rose couldn't move. She listened to him leave, just as she'd listened to him arrive. Slowly, she slid down the wall, her legs unable to support her weight any longer. Was he right? Was there hope?

Fresh tears welled in her eyes and she let them fall.

CHAPTER ELEVEN

DAVE knew he had to be careful when he dropped Melody off the following morning. It wasn't going to be easy—for either Rosie or Melody—but it was a new life and if he wanted things to work out, this was going to be the place to start.

'Is she your girlfriend?' Melody asked as they pulled up outside Reg Partridge's house, her teddy bear held securely in the crook of her arm.

Dave looked down at his daughter. 'She's a girl and, yes, she's my friend.'

'Yes, but is she your *girlfriend*?'

'How do you know about these things?' he asked, slightly bewildered. 'You're only six.'

Melody shrugged. 'Mum's had lots of boyfriends that she kisses and stuff. She said that boys have girlfriends who they kiss and that's what she was.'

Dave gritted his teeth. Mags. He should have known. He took a deep breath, not wanting to lie to his daughter. 'Rosie is a very special friend.' He met his daughter's gaze. 'And, yes, we kiss. Is that OK?'

Melody thought for a moment before shrugging. 'Guess so. I want you to stay but I know you have to go to work.'

'I'll be back later to pick you up and then we can do whatever you want.'

'Can we look for a new house?'

'Hey, that was supposed to be a surprise.'

She giggled. 'Uncle Mick said that you and I are going to be moving from the farm into a house of our very own, and that I could have a room with my own bed and I could choose the colours and toys and everything.' Her face was filled with such excited anticipation even if it *hadn't* been in his plans, he would have changed them.

'When did you speak to Uncle Mick about this?'

'This morning. I woke up just before he left.'

'That was very early.'

'Yeah.' She giggled again. 'Three o'clock! I've never been up at three o'clock in the morning before. Uncle Mick told me to go back to bed just before he drove off.'

'Good ol' Uncle Mick,' Dave muttered. He reached out and cupped her cheek with his hand. She leaned into him a little, the action warming his heart. 'You're very beautiful, Melody. So very beautiful and special.' He took a deep breath. 'But right now Daddy's going to be late for clinic if we don't get a move on.'

Melody climbed from the car and waited for him so they could walk up the path together. 'I'm sure the morning will pass quickly.' He carried the bag she'd packed. 'You've got all kinds of things to do in here.'

'I guess so.'

He knocked on the door. 'You'll have fun with Rosie.' Please! Please, let them have fun together, he silently pleaded. 'Rosie's a great cook.'

'Really? She can cook?'

'Not only that but her dad writes books that tell people *how* to cook.'

'Wow!'

The door opened and Rose stood there, looking stunning in a pair of white shorts and a red summer top, a smile pasted on her face. Dave felt his insides twist with desire at seeing her there, looking very nervous. She had guts. More than anyone else he'd met. After everything she'd been through, she was willing to keep on going. He admired that.

'Hi.' She knew she sounded overly bright but she couldn't help it.

'Good morning.'

'Come on in,' she ventured.

'Thanks. Rosie, this is Melody. Mel, this is Rosie.' Dave performed the introductions. To his surprise, Rose bent down, bringing herself to eye level with Melody.

'I'm very pleased to meet you, Melody.' The child wasn't smiling and Rose faltered for a moment. She glanced up at Dave for reassurance. He nodded so she continued. 'I'm right in the middle of cooking some biscuits. Double chocolate chip.'

'Your dad's recipe?' Dave asked, his mouth instantly watering.

'Yes.' This time when she smiled at him it was genuine. She straightened. 'Come through to the kitchen. I'm almost at the stage where I'll need some help.'

'Well, *I* can't stay,' Dave replied with disgust as he put Melody's bag down and followed Rose. 'Perhaps you could help her, Mel?'

'But I've never cooked before,' the little girl said as she hesitantly followed her father, teddy still grasped firmly in her arms.

That stumped Rose. She couldn't remember a time when she hadn't been in the kitchen, helping her father cook. 'Well, there's a first time for everything. Besides, after we've made them and cooked them, we get to eat them.'

'You'd better save some for me,' Dave warned, and she realised he was serious.

She laughed. 'We'll think about it. Now go to work.' Rose was astonished with herself. She'd been so nervous about this morning, especially after what she and Dave had discussed last night, but amazingly she felt relaxed and calm at having the six-year-old for the next four or so hours. If Melody had never cooked and was interested in learning, Rose knew how they might spend their time. It wasn't going to be so bad after all.

'All right, then,' he muttered, as he held Melody's hand and walked over to the bench. 'But promise me you'll save me at least two.'

'Promise. Now, go. We'll be fine.' As she said the words, she realised she meant them. She watched as he bent to give Melody a hug and kiss, wondering whether he was going to give her one or not.

She also heard him whisper, 'Remember, Daddy loves you.' And Rose's heart filled with love for him.

Dave stood and met Rose's gaze over his daughter's head. 'You OK?' he mouthed. She nodded and smiled. Dave smiled back and blew Rose a kiss before heading to the door.

'All right. We need to sift this flour into the bowl, Melody.' She stopped. 'Do you like being called Melody or Mel?'

'Mel,' the little girl answered. 'It's my nickname that Uncle Mick and Dad call me. Dad says that everyone has to have a nickname because then it makes them feel special.'

'I guess he's right,' Rose answered, knowing she cherished the way Dave said *her* nickname.

Dave listened for a moment and released the breath he'd been unconsciously holding. Everything *was* going to be fine. He could always count on Rosie to pull through.

Three hours later, they'd made two batches of biscuits, mainly because they'd eaten all the ones from the first batch, made an upside-down pineapple cake and started on preparations for a beef wellington Rose was cooking for dinner that night. She'd made a little apron for teddy out of a hand towel and had readjusted the straps on one for Melody. Teddy had mainly watched as Melody hadn't wanted him to get too dirty and Rose had agreed, although she was almost sure she'd seen teddy sneak a biscuit or two.

'What's in the bag?' Rose asked as she hung up the drying towel. At least the kitchen was once again clean.

'Books and stuff,' Melody replied, collecting teddy from the bench and taking off his apron.

'What kind of books? Reading books?' Perhaps Rose could read Melody a story.

'Some.' She shrugged and started pulling them out.

School books, Rose realised with a frown. Well, if Dave had sent her with work to do then she guessed they had to do it, but they could at least do it somewhere more comfortable than in the kitchen.

'Why don't we go into the lounge room and sit in there?' Rose gathered up the books and Melody followed like a dutiful puppy. Rose sat down on the floor and spread the books all over the carpet. Melody gaped openly. 'What's wrong?'

'You're sitting on the carpet.'

'Sure. Try it. It's nice and soft.'

'But carpet isn't for sitting on, chairs are. Carpet is for clean feet but not dirty shoes.'

'Really?' That sounded like something Julian would have said. 'Well, I don't have dirty shoes and neither do you. This carpet is nice and soft.' Rose patted it with her hand. 'Come and try it.'

Melody came over and sat down, a small, intrigued smile on her face.

'So, which of these books do you think we should start with?'

'I don't care.'

Rose looked up and was surprised to find Melody's smile had disappeared. 'You don't have to do this if you don't want to,' she said, touching the school books lightly. 'We can always do something else.'

'Like what?'

'Um…' Now you've done it, she thought. 'What do you *like* doing?'

Melody thought. 'I like playing with dolls. I did that once at Chelsea's house.'

'Oh? Is Chelsea a friend of yours?'

Melody shook her head. 'Not really. I don't have any friends.'

'What about the girls at school?'

Melody shook her head again. 'They're not very nice. They say mean things and that I'm a baby because of teddy and that I cried when Miss Schansky took him away from me, but I'm not a baby. I'm a big girl.' There was a hint of defiance in her eyes and Rose liked it.

'Yes, you are.'

'Really? You really think so?'

'Yes, I do.'

'Mummy always says I'm too little and to get out of her way.' Melody frowned and hugged teddy close.

'What's wrong, Mel?'

Tears trembled on the little eyelashes. 'I don't think my mummy loves me.' The tears rolled over. 'She never tells me and said I was going to live with Daddy and not her but…but my daddy loves me. He told me so.'

Rose could feel her own tears threatening. Funny, she'd thought she'd cried them all out last night. 'Yes, he does,' she concurred, and pulled a tissue from her pocket. She reached over and dabbed at Melody's eyes. 'I'll tell you something special, Mel. I know exactly how you feel.'

Six-year-old eyes widened in surprise but she didn't speak.

'My mummy didn't love me either.' Saying the words out loud hurt, but the instant they were out, Rose started to feel better. She'd done it. She'd said those hateful and horrible words out loud. 'But my daddy does. He *still* does and I'm all grown up. Your daddy will love you *just* like that, too.'

Melody took the tissue out of Rose's hand and dabbed it against Rose's eyes. The action nearly brought on a fresh bout. She took a deep breath in and said, 'Now, how about we find some dolls to play with, eh?'

Melody nodded and smiled. A *real* smile and one that Rose reciprocated.

Rose almost lost track of time and if the phone hadn't rung, she would have been late for Theatre. 'Dr Partridge,' she answered.

'Hi, Rosie. How's it going?' Dave's concern wasn't lost on her. She knew how important today had been for all of them.

'Great. Really great. She's wonderful, Dave.'

He let out the breath he'd been holding. 'That's just what I needed to hear.'

'What's up?'

'I'm running late. Can you bring Mel with you to the hospital? I'll be finished by the time you get here but I'm conscious of not making you late.'

'Sure.'

'Make sure you bring my biscuits,' he reminded her.

'Would you ever let me forget? I'll put some in for Mick as well.'

'And me,' Melody added.

'Of course. All right. We'll see you soon.' She hung up and explained to Melody. 'So we need to pack up and I need to get changed for work.'

'Will you be working all night? I thought doctors worked at night.'

'Sometimes we do but not today.' Rose helped her pack up. 'My dad and his new wife are coming back from their holiday today.'

'Your dad got married again?'

'Yes.'

'So now you have a new mum?'

'Kind of. Her name is Beverley and I don't really think of her as my mum. I think of her as my friend. A good friend who really loves my dad.'

'Margaret—that's my mum—is getting married tomorrow but she didn't want me there. Julian—that's her yucky boyfriend—doesn't like me either but I don't like him. They're going on a honeymoon and I heard Margaret saying that she'd trick Daddy into letting me stay.'

'But she didn't *need* to trick him,' Rose replied. 'Your

daddy *wants* you. Remember he told you how much he loved you?'

'Yeah.' Melody's eyes registered her statements before they dimmed again. 'But I don't ever want to get married. Yuck.'

Rose didn't have time to debate the issue and it seemed as though Melody had made up her mind at any rate. No doubt she'd change it when she got older and give her father and Uncle Mick a few grey hairs with the boyfriends she'd be bringing home.

When they arrived at the hospital, Rose was running five minutes late but she made sure she said goodbye properly to Melody.

'I've had so much fun today. Thank you for coming to play, Mel.'

'Sounds as though you two girls have had a wow of a time,' Dave commented as Rose straightened. Melody instantly held out the container that was filled with biscuits.

'Look what we made, Dad.'

Dave opened the lid and took one out, biting into it immediately. 'Mmm. You girls,' he said as he swallowed his bite, 'are such good cooks. Mmm-mmm.'

Melody giggled and on that note Rose said her goodbyes and headed to Theatre.

Thankfully, the list was routine with no surprises, which she was very relieved about because, whether it was due to her bad night's sleep or playing with Melody all morning, Rose felt completely washed out.

When she arrived back at the house, she was glad to see her father and Beverley were home, her dad back in the kitchen he loved, putting the finishing touches to the dinner she'd started earlier.

While they ate, both of them chattering about their honeymoon, Rose started to unwind but couldn't suppress the yawns that kept plaguing her. 'Sorry,' she apologised as she rose from the table.

'Go to bed, dear,' Beverley said. 'You've obviously had a busy day.'

'Thanks. I think I will.' She kissed Beverley goodnight but when she went over to her father, he held her at arm's length.

'Rosie, darling, I don't want to pry, but you know I'm here for you if you need anything. To talk and things like that. Beverley, too,' he added. 'We both care about you so much and we just want you to be happy. You can count on us.'

'I know,' she said, and gave her father a big hug. 'Everything's still kind of muddled in my head and I'm too tired to try and make sense of it.'

'Well, off you go to bed, then, princess.'

'Goodnight.' Rose headed off to her room and had just closed the door when the phone rang. She groaned and then remembered that she didn't need to worry about answering it. She waited for a moment, listening for footsteps heading her way in case there was an emergency at the hospital, but after a few minutes she continued on to the bathroom to wash before bed.

Five hours later, Rose was walking quietly through to the kitchen to make herself a drink. She'd managed to sleep but had woken with a start, unable to breathe properly, her body trembling with fright.

'You all right, dear?'

She jumped as Beverley came into the room, water flying out from the kettle she was filling.

'Sorry, I didn't mean to startle you. Can't sleep?' Beverley took the kettle from Rose. 'Sit down. I'll make us a nice warm drink.'

'It's OK, I can—'

'Sit. Your father's asleep, which means I get free run of his precious kitchen.' Beverley smiled as she spoke. Once the kettle was boiling and Beverley had set out the cups, she sat down opposite Rose. 'Now, what's going on with you and Dave?'

'Oh, Beverley.' Rose slumped forward, her head resting on the bench. 'I don't know whether I'm coming or going.'

'Do you love him?'

'Yes.'

'Do you know if he loves you?'

'He says he does. He said he wants to marry me.'

'Really!' Rose lifted her head and looked into her step-mother's astonished eyes. 'This is serious.'

'Yes.'

'So what's the problem?'

Rose wasn't quite sure where to start.

'Is it his daughter? Are you afraid to take on an im-mediate family?'

'Oh, I don't know,' Rose wailed, and slumped forward again. 'I'm just so confused. Do I change my nice quiet lifestyle to accommodate a man and his child? Am I ca-pable of that? Will I make a good mother?'

'Is that what's bothering you? Whether or not you'll turn out like your mother?'

Rose nodded. 'That's part of it. I'm just not good at taking chances, Beverley. I took a chance with Julian and look what happened.'

'But that was a wrong chance to take.'

'How am I supposed to know what's right and what's not?'

Beverley reached over and placed her hand on Rose's. 'You follow your heart.' The kettle boiled and soon Rose had a hot toddy in front of her. 'Sip it slowly. It's your father's recipe.' Beverley sat down again. 'I can tell you straight out, Rosie, that you're nothing like your mother. Oh, you may look like her, but in personality you are ex-actly like your father.'

'But how could you know? You've never—'

'Met your mother?' Beverley finished. 'Yes, I have. Of course, I had no idea she was your father's ex-wife until much later, but I knew her all right. She was my boss years ago when I lived in Sydney. She's since moved overseas to work and all I can say is good riddance to her.'

'She was in Sydney?'

'For many years.'

Rose felt even more dejected. 'She really doesn't like me, does she?' Tears stung at her eyes and Beverley quickly took her hand again.

'It's not a matter of like or dislike as far as she's concerned. She's just...' Beverley shrugged '...indifferent. Not that I'm making excuses for her.' She paused. 'I know this is easy to say and hard to do, but try not to take it personally, dear. She was indifferent to everyone she met. She has no real friends, no real relationships, except with her company, but that's who she is. So, you see, you are *nothing* like her. You aren't an icicle nor an emotional nomad. You're a woman on the brink of self-discovery, deciding whether to trust herself as well as trust others with her heart.'

Rose sipped at her drink, taking in what her stepmother had said.

'I can understand your reluctance because your father was the same. I knew from the moment I first met him, when we were discussing the photo layout for his first book, that I wanted to marry him.'

'But that was almost ten years ago.'

'That's right. Don't waste ten years of your life, Rosie. As soon as you know, do it. Get on with it now. So what if things have happened quickly? They've happened! If you love Dave, then take the chance. Trust your instincts. Listen to your heart. From what Dave has said, it seems Melody had a lovely time this morning, which proves you're nothing like your mother.'

'Dave? You've spoken to Dave?'

Beverley nodded. 'He called just as you were heading to bed. He wants me to look after Melody when he's working. I looked after her last time she came to stay and told

Dave I'd do the same whenever she came back. She's such a gorgeous child.'

Rose couldn't resist the smile that tugged at her lips when she thought of Melody. 'Yes, she is. I didn't realise you'd looked after her before.'

'Oh, yes. Moving to Broken Hill is just what Melody needs—get her away from her mother. Fancy sending a child all the way here from Sydney on her own! Poor darling. Thank goodness Dave has sense, so he called tonight to take me up on my earlier offer to help.' Beverley had a twinkle of excitement in her eyes as she continued. 'We'll fix up the spare room for her in case he works late at the hospital or has an emergency and Melody needs to stay the night. Apparently she loved cooking with you today and can't wait to do some more. Reg is looking forward to having another little girl in his kitchen, one he can pamper and teach—so it works out well for everyone.'

'It all seems well organised, then.'

'Nearly. There's one thing missing from the equation. You! Don't let this opportunity pass you by, Rosie.' Beverley squeezed her hand. 'Reach out and grab that happiness. It's just sitting there. Waiting for you. You'll be a wonderful mother for Melody and the perfect wife for Dave.'

'What if it's too late? What if he's changed his mind? What if he's decided all he needs is Melody? What if he doesn't want me any more?'

'Oh, I doubt that, dear. I doubt that very much. You know what to do. All you have to do is to follow your heart.'

The next day, Rose woke late and couldn't believe the time. 'Half past twelve!' She jumped out of bed and quickly showered. Before she'd gone back to sleep, she'd made a vow to find Dave and ask him to marry her.

Beverley was right. She had to trust her instincts and her heart. He wasn't Julian and she wasn't her mother.

They had a chance at happiness—all three of them—and she wasn't going to let it pass her by!

'Good morning,' her father said as she entered the kitchen. 'Or should I say good afternoon?'

'You shouldn't have let me sleep so late,' she told him, after kissing his cheek. She quickly poured herself a glass of orange juice and drank it, before picking up her car keys.

'I didn't want to wake you. Where are you going?'

Rose blew him a kiss. 'To ask Dave to marry me,' she said, before heading out to her car. She was running on nervous energy and as she drove out to his farm it occurred to her that he might not be there. It was the first time she'd been out that way and, after glancing at the map book a few times and doing two U-turns, she finally found it.

There were no cars in front of the house, and with the absence of Dave's ute she guessed he wasn't around. Still, she climbed out and knocked on the door but wasn't surprised when no one answered.

'The hospital,' she said, and turned the car in that direction. Again, his ute wasn't in the car park and she didn't fancy going in and asking the nurses if they knew where he was. Where else could he be? Doing house calls? Looking at houses? Visiting friends? Grocery shopping? He could be anywhere in Broken Hill or its outskirts.

She thought hard and then snapped her fingers. 'The pub.' She'd try the pub he liked, and if he wasn't there, she'd simply wait until someone turned up who knew where he was. 'You're not giving in,' she told herself sternly. 'You're going to be engaged to Dave Dunbar by the end of this day or else!'

Her hopes plummeted when she pulled into the pub car park, noticing Dave's ute was absent from there as well. She sighed as she locked up her car and headed inside. The cool air hit her and she pushed her sunglasses up to the top of her head, searching the room for the man she loved.

'G'day, Rosie,' one of the nurses called, and beckoned her over. 'How's it going?'

'Good,' Rose replied in response to the typical Australian greeting.

'Rosie.' The deep voice behind her made her heart race and she turned expectantly.

'G'day, Mick,' she murmured a moment later, her face falling.

Mick laughed. 'You've got it bad, Rosie. Real bad.'

Rose was conscious of the people around them watching her closely. 'Uh…do you know where your brother is?' she asked him quietly, hoping everyone wouldn't hear.

Mick frowned. 'Dave? Not sure. Hey!' He called at the top of his lungs. 'Has anyone seen Dave? Rosie's looking for him.'

Rose could feel herself blushing but she watched as nearly everyone shook their heads, wide grins spreading across their faces.

'Sorry. What did you want him for? Can I pass on a message?'

Rose swallowed over the lump in her throat. 'Um…er…no. I guess I'll catch up with him later.' Rose took her sunglasses off her head and was about to put them back on when Mick took her arm.

'Don't go. Stay and have a drink.' He ushered her to a table and sat down opposite her.

Rose eyed him carefully. 'Why? Why do you want me to stay?' When Mick didn't answer, she nodded slowly. 'You *do* know where he is, don't you?'

'And if I do?'

'Then tell me.'

Mick looked thoughtfully at her. 'How about we arm-wrestle for it?'

'Arm-wrestle? For what?'

'For the information.'

'What?' She frowned at him, puzzled, but his words had

stopped conversations around them and people were listening in unashamedly.

'If you win, I'll tell you where Dave is.'

'And if you win?' she queried, not sure she liked this idea at all.

'Then you have to tell me whether or not you love my brother.'

'*What?* That's none of your business.'

'That's the deal, Rosie.'

'But you'll win easily. That's not very fair.'

He nodded. 'You can use two hands.'

'Two—'

'Go on, Rosie,' one of the nurses encouraged her. 'You can take him.'

'Yeah, go on, Rosie.' Cheers went up around the place and Mick put his elbow down on the table, his palm open, waiting for hers.

Rose glanced over at the door, wondering how fast she could run. The cheering around them was starting to become louder and she even saw people passing money, placing bets.

'Come on, Rosie. You can do it, girl,' people chanted from the sidelines. 'He's a weakling. You can take him.'

Mick looked far from a weakling but as she could see no way out, she put her arm on the table, mirroring Mick's position. He clasped her hand in his and waited for the count.

'Three, two, one—go!' someone shouted, and Rose felt the instant pressure of Mick's muscles. She brought her other hand up and started to push the other way. If she lost, she'd have to confess to all these people here that she loved Dave, but if she won, then she could speak to him in private. She wrestled as though her life depended on it.

Putting all her weight behind it, Rose pushed harder and almost had Mick's hand to the table when a movement in her peripheral vision caused her to look away.

Dave! He was standing there. Watching them. Scowling

at her. Melody was by his side, holding onto his hand. Even with the scowl, the sight of him warmed her heart and made her mind go blank. She felt her heart rate increase and started to feel a little light-headed.

'Yeah!' Mick crowed, as he managed to bend her arms backwards. Everyone clapped and cheered and Rose returned her attention to what had just happened. 'All right, Rosie. Pay up.'

Before she could utter a word, Dave let go of Melody's hand, stormed over and wrenched his brother out of the chair. 'What are you doing?' he demanded roughly. 'Are you out of your mind? You could have hurt her.'

Mick grinned stupidly at his brother and Rose realised Mick wasn't at all bothered by Dave's protective behaviour. 'It's all in your honour, bro'.'

'What are you talking about?' Dave held firmly onto the collar of his brother's shirt.

'Tell him, Rosie. Time to pay up.'

Rose stood, swallowing the enormous lump that was lodged in her throat. Everyone around them went quiet.

She stared at Dave, meeting his gaze, knowing this was the man she wanted to spend the rest of her life with.

Taking a deep breath, she said clearly, 'I love you.'

Dave's gaze remained on hers as he dropped his brother's shirt. No one moved or spoke, all eyes now anxiously on Dave to see how he would react. He didn't have to say anything, not as far as Rose was concerned.

She knew that by coming here and confessing her love for him, it was sealing their future in the sweetest way possible. He'd already said that he loved her and wanted to marry her, and she was certain, by the desire that flared in the blue depths of his eyes, that he still felt that way.

Both of them stood, frozen, content just to look at each other, their hearts communicating in a language as old as time.

Dave couldn't believe it. Rosie loved him. He'd been

certain of it but to actually hear her say the words was…incredible. Like a dream come true.

He felt a little hand slip inside his and he glanced down at his daughter. Melody nodded at him then reached out and slipped her other hand through Rosie's—uniting the three of them together.

'Perfect,' Dave said softly. 'Just perfect.'

EPILOGUE

'COME on,' Dave called, as he hoisted Melody up into his arms. 'All unmarried men and women in the centre of the room.'

Rose smiled brightly at her new husband as he held out his free hand for her. She kissed the father of the bride on the cheek before heading over to Dave's side, her cream-coloured wedding gown shimmering and sparkling as she walked.

Melody's dress was made from the same material, except for a red sash around her waist which matched the colour of Beverley's matron-of-honour dress.

'Unmarried men on that side.' Dave sectioned the room off. 'Unmarried women on the other.'

Everyone was laughing and joking as people shuffled into their places. Rose was having such a wonderful day, especially as all her dreams had come true. She smiled at her new stepdaughter, now content in the knowledge that she and Melody had taken the time during the last six months to really get to know each other. She never would have thought a six-year-old girl would be one of her best friends.

'All right, princess,' Dave said softly to Melody. 'Throw the garter first.'

'Do you think she'll get him?' Rose asked quietly.

'She should do. We've been practising her throwing skills for the past month or so,' Dave mumbled. 'Can you see Uncle Mick, Mel?'

'Yep.'

'Then let's count to three.' Dave cleared his throat.

'Ready?' he called. 'One, two, three!' Melody took aim over her father's shoulder and threw the garter.

'Yes!' She punched the air with her fist. 'It got him, Dad.'

Dave and Rose turned to look. They both laughed as Mick twirled the garter around his index finger and everyone clapped.

'Ready for the next one, Mel?' Rose asked.

'Sure. This is fun.'

'All right, ladies,' Rose called. 'One, two, three!' Melody threw the bouquet over Rose's shoulder, making sure it landed firmly in Mick's girlfriend's arms.

'Woo-hoo!' she called. 'I did it.'

Dave and Rose turned to look again as Mick stared at his girlfriend. Everyone was laughing and cheering.

'Excellent throwing, Mel.' Dave kissed his daughter.

'Couldn't have done it better myself. I'm proud of you, too.' Rose kissed Melody's other cheek. The girl between them giggled happily.

They all looked at Mick who was still staring at his girlfriend, his jaw hanging open in disbelief.

'Ah, face facts, bro',' Dave called. 'The garter and flower toss never lie. Rose and I are proof of it.'

Rose leaned over and kissed her new husband on the lips. 'Absolutely, my love. Absolutely.'

Modern Romance™
...seduction and
passion guaranteed

Tender Romance™
...love affairs that
last a lifetime

Sensual Romance™
...sassy, sexy and
seductive

Blaze Romance™
...the temperature's
rising

Medical Romance™
...medical drama on
the pulse

Historical Romance™
...rich, vivid and
passionate

27 new titles every month.

*With all kinds of Romance for
every kind of mood...*

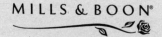

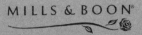

MILLS & BOON®

Medical Romance™

DEAR DOCTOR *by Meredith Webber*

Kirsten is engaged — sort of — to handsome rancher
Grant. So what if playboy paediatrician Josh Phillips
broke her heart? She's over it — and over him.
Kirsten wants commitment, the one thing Josh can't
give her. So why has her engagement done nothing at
all for Kirsten's heart...and punched a hole in Josh's?

SURGEON ON CALL *by Alison Roberts*

Joe Petersen is a skilled surgeon — unfortunately,
when it comes to being a dad he's a complete
amateur! Joe's working with emergency consultant
Fliss Munroe, and he wants her to be more than a
colleague. What better way to get her interest than
to recruit her to plan the best ever birthday party for
a five-year-old girl!

THE DOCTOR'S ADOPTION WISH
by Gill Sanderson

When Nurse Jane Hall returns from California to
help Dr Cal Mitchell take care of their orphaned
niece, his life, his plans and his emotions are thrown
into disarray. Jane might be a wanderer at heart,
but Keldale is her home — and if Cal could only admit
that he's fallen in love with her she just might stay
for ever...

On sale 7th February 2003

Available from 17th January 2003

*Available at most branches of WH Smith,
Tesco, Martins, Borders, Eason, Sainsbury's
and all good paperback bookshops.*

0203/24/MB62

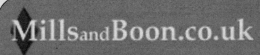

2 FREE

books and a surprise gift!

We would like to take this opportunity to thank you for reading this Mills & Boon® book by offering you the chance to take TWO more specially selected titles from the Historical Romance™ series absolutely FREE! We're also making this offer to introduce you to the benefits of the Reader Service™—

- ★ FREE home delivery
- ★ FREE gifts and competitions
- ★ FREE monthly Newsletter
- ★ Exclusive Reader Service discount
- ★ Books available before they're in the shops

Accepting these FREE books and gift places you under no obligation to buy, you may cancel at any time, even after receiving your free shipment. Simply complete your details below and return the entire page to the address below. *You don't even need a stamp!*

YES! Please send me 2 free Historical Romance books and a surprise gift. I understand that unless you hear from me, I will receive 4 superb new titles every month for just £3.49 each, postage and packing free. I am under no obligation to purchase any books and may cancel my subscription at any time. The free books and gift will be mine to keep in any case.

H3ZEA

Ms/Mrs/Miss/Mr ....Initials....................................
                                                      BLOCK CAPITALS PLEASE

Surname ....

Address ....

....

....Postcode................................

Send this whole page to:
UK: FREEPOST CN81, Croydon, CR9 3WZ
EIRE: PO Box 4546, Kilcock, County Kildare (stamp required)